ACCESS POINT

Tom Gabbay

First Printing, 2020
ISBN: 978-0-578-67388-2

JMS BOOKS
London, United Kingdom

www.tomgabbay.com

For My Other Half...

When we look into the night sky and see a star that ceased to exist many millions of years ago, we are looking into the past.

Some memories never die.

Prologue.

"Are you ready?"

The subject took a deep breath and nodded. Ula could sense his anxiety, but the man's emotional state was of no interest to her. In fact, it was a bit annoying.

"You need to empty your mind of all extraneous thoughts," she said, placing the E.I.R. onto his head. Fashioned out of an old bicycle helmet, the unit held eighteen transmitters in key locations within the padding, each one connected to a colour-coded wire, all of which came together in a cable that led to the mainframe computer. Not unlike the connection between a laptop and a printer, except that in this case, the printer would be a human brain.

The man reached down to stroke the guide dog that sat patiently at his side. An unwelcome distraction, Ula instructed him to keep his hands folded together in his lap.

"I'm sorry," the man apologised. "I'm a bit nervous."

It wasn't a question so Ula didn't bother with a reply. Taking her place at the station, she opened the programme and brought the four GIFs she'd created to the front of the screen. Simple animations drawn in crisp, white lines on an empty black background, there was a hummingbird, a kite, a galloping horse, and a boy on a bicycle. Easy to code and, if the trial was successful, easy to recognise and describe.

"I'm going to begin now," she said after running a final systems check. "Please lean your head back onto the pillow and imagine that you're lying in a field of grass, staring upwards into a deep, dark void. Focus on it and nothing else, but don't try too hard. Let it come to you. The first image will be generated in three... two... one..."

The man drew a shaky breath and held it, his pulse rising as his heart beat wildly in anticipation.

"A positive result is more likely if you relax," Ula said. "Please breathe normally."

He exhaled and tried to focus on the dark world that enveloped him, searching for something, anything, but finding only the uninterrupted emptiness that he'd lived with for three of his six decades. His hopes were starting to fade when a sudden streak of soft white light broke through the veil. But like a silent flash of faraway lightning, it was gone as quickly as it appeared.

Ula made a note of involuntary movement in the subject's ocular region. "Please tell me if you experience anything unusual," she said.

"I... I don't know." The man furrowed his brow. "I can't be sure... I thought I might have, but..."

"Describe what you thought you saw."

"I'm not sure if it was real." His face became contorted and his head moved reflexively from side to side, as if searching for the phantom light. "I... I can't be certain."

"Please describe it," Ula persisted.

"It was a light... very faint, like a flash... or a pulse."

"Do you still see it?" A camera was recording the session, but Ula made notes anyway. It helped her to think.

"No, it's... It's gone now. Perhaps I -- " He froze in mid-sentence. "Oh god..." His voice dropped to a whisper. "Yes, I... I see it now, but it's..."

Ula leaned forward. "What do you see?"

A wave of emotion engulfed the man, rendering him speechless. He choked on his words and started to tear up.

"Please describe what you're experiencing," Ula said, her voice rising with frustration. But the man was lost, unresponsive. She had no choice but to end the test and remove the E.I.R. from his head.

"It's very important that you tell me exactly what you saw," she said sternly. "Please describe it to me in detail."

"It was a... a bird," he was finally able to say. "Rather, a rendering of a bird. A hummingbird..." He needed to draw a breath before he could continue. "It was hovering... out there in the darkness, and I... It seemed so real... I felt I could have reached out and touched it."

He broke down and started to cry uncontrollably, upsetting his animal and making it impossible to continue. Ula had no choice but to dismiss the subject with instructions to return the following day.

After completing her notes, she locked the office and headed for the institute's empty back stairway, preferring the eight flight walk to the lift, where she would undoubtedly be forced to share the tiny space with a bunch of strangers. The experience could traumatise her for hours, sometimes for days.

Exiting into the courtyard, where her bicycle was locked to the black iron railings at the side of the building, she tried to analyse her state of mind. Something like nine years had passed since she'd written that first line of code. A quarter of her life spent gathering data, writing, testing, failing, then gathering more data, re-writing, and testing again. She'd been caught in a vicious cycle, feeling that she was getting closer with each revolution, but never quite getting there. Until now.

Why then did she feel so empty inside?

Something had changed -- something unsettling -- but she couldn't put her finger on what exactly was troubling her. In all the time she'd spent pursuing success, she'd never quite considered the consequences of achieving it.

A light rain was starting to fall as she pulled into rush hour traffic on Old Street, heading west. My god, she thought, allowing herself a private little smile. She had literally made a blind man see! Not quite a miracle, but the world would look at it that way. And there lay the problem. Once her achievement became public knowledge, everything would change. The anonymity she enjoyed within the organisation was about to come to an abrupt and very unwelcome end. They'd left her alone for ten years, but they'd all want to be part of it now.

Shifting into high gear, she pulled out of the bicycle lane and manoeuvred around a slow-moving lorry. The rain was coming down hard now and the roads were building up to the usual late afternoon gridlock. Ula kept moving, weaving in and out of traffic as she entered the Old Street roundabout, then accelerating onto City Road, heading toward Angel. When somebody honked, she turned around to give them the finger.

And that was it. She never saw the bus that left her broken and bleeding on the cold, wet concrete.

1.

In spite of living in London for a year and a month, Mia Fraser hadn't seen much of the city outside the West End and East Putney, where she'd been sharing a two bedroom flat with three other girls. Still, something about Highbury Fields was eerily familiar. The children's playground, the local pub, even the sunbathers, scattered across the green under a clear blue September sky. It all struck a chord.

Shrugging it off as an effect of too much Saturday night partying, Mia re-checked the text to confirm that she had the right address. Can't be, she thought. Too good to be true. The imposing three-story brick townhouse was not only a five-minute walk from the Victoria Line, and ten minutes to trendy Upper Street, it also sat at the exact centre of the crescent, overlooking the wide open spaces of the park. Steeling herself for disappointment, she climbed the steps to the front entrance and rang the doorbell.

"Hi!" She flashed her most charming smile when the door opened a crack. "I'm Mia."

The woman stared out at her, perplexed.

"We texted this morning... About the room?"

"Oh... The room."

Caught in the direct sunlight, the woman looked pale and drawn, older than her thirty-eight years. She had short-cropped dark hair, which she clearly cut herself, and a tall, angular frame that was hidden under a loose-fitting jumper and baggy tracksuit bottoms. She gripped a walking stick in her right hand.

"Is it still available?" Mia asked.

The woman nodded. "Yes. It's available."

"Great! I mean, I thought somebody would've snapped it up by now. It's such an amazing location!"

The woman hesitated, as if unsure how to respond, then asked, "Do you want to see it?"

"Yes, absolutely! I mean, if it's a convenient time."

She was beckoned through the door, into a dark entrance hall with an elaborately painted tile floor. The woman gestured toward a wide wooden staircase.

"It's up there," she said.

Mia was someone who couldn't stop talking when she was nervous or excited and, at the moment, she was both. "I'm American," she explained as the woman led the way to the first floor landing, supporting her weight on the cane as she painstakingly pulled herself up, step by step. "But you probably figured that out. I grew up in Franklin, Tennessee, which is pretty close to Nashville, but I've been in London for a year now, in a flat share. We just heard the landlord's selling the building so we have to get out by the end of next week, which is pretty inconvenient because that's when college starts. I'm doing a degree in Fine Arts at Central Saint Martin's. Painting. This'll be my second year. Did I say my name is Mia?"

"Yes, you did."

"Right. I thought I did but I wasn't sure. What's yours?"

"Ula." She glanced back but didn't quite look Mia in the eye.

"It's a great house," Mia said, soaking it up. "Loads of character. I love all the art."

"This is it." Ula opened the first door on the right as they stepped off the landing. "It's quite small."

Furnished with a single bed, a wardrobe, a chair, and a set of drawers, it wasn't at all small compared to what Mia was used to. There was even a window with a view across the park.

"It's perfect!" she said. "I don't have much stuff. Just a couple of suitcases and my drawing board. I'd be at school most of the day and I don't play loud music. In fact, I'm really quiet. You wouldn't even know I'm here!"

Ula pointed down the hall. "There's a separate bathroom for this room. I have my own."

"I love it. I mean I *really* love it!" Mia wondered how it could still be available. Eighty pounds a week in a location like this? It was like hitting the jackpot. "Have you had a lot of people look at it?" she asked.

"Just you."

"Really?"

Ula frowned. "Why would I lie?"

"No, I just meant... I thought you'd get dozens of people from your ad."

"Oh. I don't know. My phone's been off most of the day."

"Yeah? Well, lucky me!" Mia displayed her charming smile again. "For a change!"

"It used to be my room," Ula said. "Before my mother died."

"Oh. I'm so sorry."

Ula met Mia's eyes for the first time. "It was a long time ago," she said.

"Oh, well... I'm still sorry."

Ula seemed at a loss for what to say next, so Mia kept talking. "Do you want me to fill out an application? Or I can give you a deposit... Unless you want references first?"

"No," Ula looked away and shook her head. "You seem fine."

"Really? Oh my god, that's great! And I promise you won't regret it. I'll be the perfect housemate!"

2.

"Are you fucking kidding me?"

Mia hadn't given her best friend, Kat, any details about the new accommodation, so when they pulled up in front of the house on Highbury Crescent, she was appropriately blown away.

"You're actually going to live here?"

"Not bad, huh?"

"Jesus, it's a goddamned mansion! On the freaking park!"

"There's a view from my room."

"For eighty quid a week?"

"Yep."

"Okay, you're lying to me, right? You've got some rich sugar daddy tucked away back in America who's doling out to save you from the slums of East Putney. That's it, isn't it?"

"Nope," Mia gloated. "Poor as dirt, but lucky. For a change."

Kat's beat-up old Mini had just barely been able to fit Mia's two cases, a box of art books, her portfolio, and her drawing board, and then only when she put the top down. With no other options anywhere near the house, Kat pulled into a "Residents Only" parking bay.

"Let's live dangerously," she laughed.

Mia hesitated before slipping the key into the door. "You think I should ring first?"

"Did you pay yet?"

"A month in advance."

"Then go ahead. You officially live here."

The house was eerily still and quiet, the only illumination a single ray of sunlight that cut through the air from somewhere above, revealing a river of tiny particles floating on the otherwise invisible current. The girls looked at each other, both suddenly feeling like intruders.

"Hello...?" Mia called out softly, then a bit louder. "Anybody home?"

"Maybe she's gone out." Kat opened the door to the drawing room and peeked inside. "Look at this," she said, taking in the dusty old furnishings and heavy velvet drapes pulled tight over the bay windows. "It's like a museum in here."

"Maybe we should come back later." Mia grabbed her friend's arm and pulled her out of the room. "I don't feel right snooping around."

"There's no way I can come back later, Mia. I've got shit to do. And you're not snooping around, you're exploring your new house. Anyway, it's perfect. We can get your stuff in without her watching over us. Come on." She headed back out the door. "Before she gets back."

The drawing board was the most awkward item to move, so they left it for last. Correctly judging herself to be the stronger of the two, Kat took the bottom end, supporting the heavy piece up the stairs while the more delicate Mia navigated the steps.

"Christ, what is this thing made of?" Kat groaned. "It's fucking heavy!"

"Wanna rest?"

"No, don't stop! We'll never get there if we lose momentum!"

"Be careful of the walls."

Kat grimaced. "You know I love you, sweetie, but if you say that again I'm gonna have to seriously mess you up."

They managed to safely manoeuvre the piece onto the landing and through the doorway, into Mia's room, without causing any damage. "Where do you want it?" Kat asked.

"Well, the light's good by the window and it'd be cool to have a view of the park while I work. But maybe there's more space by the door. What do you think?"

"I honestly don't give a shit, babe, but once I put it down I'm not picking it up again."

"Okay, by the window."

"Right..."

Kat looked up and gasped. Dropping her end of the table, it hit the wooden floor with a loud *BANG!* Mia spun around and found Ula standing in the doorway.

"Ula! ... Hi!... I... I didn't see you there!"

Ula didn't reply.

"I'm, ah... We're moving in," Mia stuttered. "But I guess you can see that. Oh... This is my friend, Kat. She's helping me out."

Kat gave her a smile and a little wave. Ula nodded back, but just barely.

"We're almost done," Mia said, doing her best to recover. "This is the last thing."

Ula stayed focused on Kat for a beat too long, then turned back to Mia. "You left the front door open," she said stonily.

"Oh, my god, did we? I'm so sorry!"

Ula held her hand out and displayed a key. "And you left this in it."

"Oh, Ula, I'm really, really sorry." She stepped forward and sheepishly retrieved the key. "It won't happen again, I promise."

Ula nodded, stole a last glance at Kat, then walked off toward the back of the house.

There was, of course, a parking ticket attached to the Mini's windscreen. "Bastards," Kat moaned.

Mia reached for it. "I'll pay it."

"Forget it." Kat grabbed the ticket, crumpled it into a ball, and threw it into the back seat. "The car's registered to my dead uncle in Liverpool."

"Really?"

Kat shrugged. "My dad's idea. He said the car would give up the ghost before they could figure out that Uncle George already had."

"Your dad sounds interesting."

"That's one way to put it."

"Anyway," Mia gave her friend a hug. "I owe you one."

"And don't think I'm gonna let you forget it."

It was starting to rain so they raised the top, then Kat slipped in behind the wheel. Mia leaned onto the window.

"I'm sorry we won't be flatmates any more," she said.

"Yeah, me too."

"But we'll still see each other, right? You can come down on weekends for a sleepover."

Kat frowned. "I'm not sure that's gonna work."

"Why not?"

"Didn't you see the look she gave me?"

"She was just annoyed about the key."

"I don't know." Kat looked toward the house, then back at Mia. "She's a bit on the weird side."

"You don't know anything about her."

"Neither do you."

Mia put on a playful scowl. "You're the one who's weird!"

"Of course I am." She keyed the engine and put the car in gear. "That's why you love me."

"That's actually true."

"Are you gonna be all right?"

"Of course! I'll make friends with her."

Kat gave her a look. "Good luck with that."

Mia stepped back onto the pavement and waved as the car pulled away. "Call me!" she said, but the car was already half-way down the block.

As the Mini disappeared, Mia stood there a moment, taking in her new surroundings. There was nothing out of the ordinary - - a van parked on the kerb while the driver made a delivery; a young mother pushing a stroller; a couple of dogs chasing each other across the open field. Everything in its place, where it should be. Still. Something didn't feel right. Something felt very much out of place.

Laughing at her own foolishness, she took a deep breath and headed back into the house.

3.

Mia stood back and surveyed the room. Not bad for a couple of hours work. She'd put her clothes away, made the bed with the flowery linen her mother had given her when she left home, hung her two favourite efforts from life painting class, wrapped the battery-powered fairy lights around the mirror, and placed "Teddy" atop the set of drawers, where he could keep an eye on her, as he had for the last nineteen years. Remembering the bag of groceries she'd picked up that morning, she decided to make herself a cup of peppermint tea and get under the covers for an early night.

Tip-toeing down the stairs, she couldn't help thinking how ironic it was. Back in East Putney she was always complaining -- if not out loud, then to herself -- about the constant noise that made it impossible to think, let alone get any work done. Now she missed the music and laughter, and even the arguing that had filled that small space.

The kitchen was at the back of the house, big enough to accommodate a long wooden table at the centre of the room and a well-worn armchair in the corner, beside the wood burning stove. Surrounded on three sides by an old formica countertop and worn out painted cupboards, on the back wall there was a blue door that Mia guessed would lead down to the cellar. Perhaps there was a utility room with a washer and dryer down there, like at home. She gave it a try, but it was locked.

Aside from some old cheese, a half-eaten banana, and a box of Cheerios, the fridge was completely empty. Mia added a dozen eggs, a litre of milk, and a six-pack of plain yogurt pots before turning the kettle on. The cupboard was better stocked, with a half-dozen tins of tuna, about the same number of soup cans, a box of PG tips, a jar of Marmite, and several boxes of water biscuits. By the time the kettle boiled Mia had organised her things on the shelf above, and washed out a teacup.

Balancing the hot drink as she headed back up the hallway toward the stairs, she noticed the drawing room door was ajar. Curious, she pushed it open a crack, but found only pitch black. Locating a switch near the door, she flicked it on, filling the room with a soft, incandescent light.

The air was stale, the carpets musty, and the dark mahogany furniture was covered in a layer of thin white dust. Mia was drawn to the far end of the room, where a group of three photos stood in tarnished silver frames atop a grand piano. Placing her cup on a side table, she picked up the first frame which was a black and white shot depicting a young woman in a white lab coat posing outside an institutional-looking building. In her mid-twenties, the woman was tall and slender with straight dark hair, high cheekbones, and a delicate jawline. Her thin lips were un-painted but her eyebrows were drawn in two thick black lines arched across her forehead. On closer inspection, Mia could see that something had been scrawled in pen across the lower righthand corner of the picture. The year, 1974, was clear, but the rest was written in what Mia thought might be the Russian alphabet.

The second photo, in washed out colour, featured the same woman, but this time she was standing on Highbury Crescent, with the house behind her. A few years older, she stood expressionless, tightly gripping a pram that held two seemingly identical infants. Perhaps eighteen months old, the children sat side-by-side in matching outfits, both staring intensely at the camera, as did their mother.

The final photograph showed the woman with a group of men, all standing in front of a blackboard that had a very long, complicated equation written on it. The men, wearing white shirts and ties but not jackets, were all smiles while the woman, who stood slightly apart from the group, gazed stony-eyed at some unseen object beyond the photographer.

"Don't look at that!"

Mia gasped and swung around, knocking her teacup off the table.

"Oh, my god, I..."

She stopped in mid-sentence because no one was there. She was alone in the room. Confused, she went to the door and peeked out into the hallway. There was no sign of anyone, and the house was completely silent. Eerily silent. Had Ula been there and disappeared? How could she vanish so quickly? Mia started to wonder if she'd actually heard anything at all. She was tired and on edge, nervous about her first night in the big house. Maybe she'd imagined it. In fact, now that she thought about it, the voice did seem a bit unreal. Faint and hollow, as if emanating from some faraway place. Like a dream.

After gathering up the scattered pieces of her broken cup and mopping up the peppermint tea, Mia headed back upstairs with the intention of getting straight into bed. It was natural, she told herself, to feel a bit strange in a new, unfamiliar environment. Things would soon get back to normal. She resolved to spend some quality time with Ula in the coming days. The better they got to know each other, the easier it would be for them both to make the adjustment.

As she reached the top of the stairs, Mia paused, thinking she heard another faraway voice. But this time, instead of evaporating into thin air, it persisted. Muted and indistinct, but unquestionably real, it sounded like two voices having a whispered conversation.

Following the sound to the back of the house, she paused at Ula's bedroom. The door was wide open, revealing a space at least twice the size of her own room. From her vantage point in the hallway, she could see the bottom half of a king-sized four poster bed, unmade, and, on the wall, a widescreen television that was playing electronic noise. A few articles of clothing were scattered around the room and there was a dead plant in the corner. But no voices.

There was another door at the end of the hallway, smaller and narrower than the others in the house. Although open only a crack, Mia could see that a set of narrow wooden stairs led up, presumably to an attic. The voices, more distinct now, were certainly coming from there. Mia leaned in to listen.

"It's not at all clear..." a man said in what sounded like a German accent. "There's too much interference."

Mia recognised Ula's voice responding, but she was quieter, more difficult to understand than the German. She said something about "polarity."

"Yes..." the German replied after a moment. "That's much better. In fact, it's very good. A very clear seven. Try another..." It was a moment before he spoke again. "Yes, excellent," he said. "Twelve. And another? Yes, forty-eight. No, wait, it's a three. Forty-three."

Straining to hear, Mia leaned too hard against the door and it shut with a loud *CLICK*. The man went suddenly silent and a moment later, heavy footsteps were coming down the stairs. Mia raced down the hallway, slipped into her room, and eased the door shut. She stood there listening, not daring to breath, as the attic door opened and the man stepped out into the hallway. He took a few steps toward her room, then stopped and retraced his steps back up the hall. Mia didn't exhale until she heard the door close and the footsteps fade as the man climbed the steps back up to the attic.

Being extra careful not to make a sound, she reached down and slowly turned the key in her door, locking herself into the room.

4.

The alarm slowly pierced her consciousness, interrupting a deep, dark, empty slumber. She opened her eyes, but didn't move, not at first. She just lay there, staring up at the ceiling, trying to piece things together. Where exactly was she? Had she been dreaming? Was she dreaming now?

Propping herself up on one elbow, the world started to come into focus. She picked up the phone, swiped the screen, and found a message from Kat:

> sleep well, doll? 🙀🙀 up and at 'em! 🌼🌼
>
> hey, let's do lunch!!! xxx 😘

It made Mia smile, which was more often than not the effect Kat had on her. They'd met a year earlier, on moving-in day at the East Putney flat, and had quickly bonded. Kat, from up north somewhere, was new to London, too, but being a couple of years older and considerably more street smart than the small town girl, it was natural for her to take the American under her wing. Mia was sorry to lose her as a flatmate, but it all happened so fast and Kat was able to move in with some friends from home who had a house in Tooting.

Employed in the makeup department at Marks and Spencer on Oxford Street, Kat would get the tube to King's Cross a couple times a week to meet Mia for lunch in the school caf. The food was cheap and she seemed to appreciate the off-beat atmosphere of the art school, probably a welcome break from selling foundation to pimply teenagers.

Mia tapped out a reply:

it's a date... and i'm buying! 😇😇 💜

There was no response, but it was almost nine o'clock so Kat would be on the underground by now. Mia slipped out of bed, threw some clothes on, and headed for the bathroom. The sun was shining and, after her long sleep, she felt regenerated. And hungry.

She was startled to find a man sitting at the kitchen table, eating a large plate of scrambled eggs as he perused his iPad.

"Oh," she said, stopping in the doorway. "Hi."

The man looked up and gave her a weary look. In his mid-forties, he was handsome, in a disheveled, scholarly sort of way. "You must be the lodger," he said in a German accent.

"Um... Yeah... I guess I am."

He nodded. "What's your name?"

"Mia."

"Mia what?"

"Mia Fraser."

He nodded again and went back to his iPad. "Help yourself to the eggs," he said without looking up. "I thought Ula was going to eat something but apparently not."

Mia looked over at the stove and saw that half her box of eggs had been cracked open. She found a plate and served herself.

"What's yours?" she said as she sat down.

"What?"

"Your name. I told you mine, but you didn't tell me yours."

"Erik Berg," he said.

Mia ate a couple of bites then put her fork down. The eggs were overcooked and cold. "Where is Ula anyway?" she asked, trying to sound nonchalant.

"Sleeping," he replied. "We were at it all night."

"Oh."

He looked up and frowned. "I didn't mean we were having sex."

"No, I didn't think -- "

"We were working," he said, going back to the screen.

"Right." Mia got up and surreptitiously dumped the rest of her eggs into the bin. "What kind of work do you do?" she asked.

"Bio-technical neurology."

"Ah." She filled the kettle and turned it on. "I guess that doesn't mean a lot to me."

"It doesn't to most people."

"Sounds interesting, though."

"It can be."

He clearly wanted her to shut up, but she decided to give it one more try. "How do you know Ula?"

Erik gave her a look. "You ask a lot of questions."

"Sorry."

He took his glasses off and breathed a long sigh. "We work together."

"Oh. Would you like a cup of peppermint tea?"

"Yes, all right." He showed something that passed for a smile, then put his glasses back on and went back to his reading.

As Mia waited for the kettle to boil she started to feel a bit uneasy. It was that same feeling she'd had a day earlier, a vague sensation that somebody was watching her. But it was stronger this time, as if someone was right there, behind her, breathing down her neck. She tried to dismiss it, but it was impossible to ignore.

"Is something wrong?" Erik asked.

"No, I... I'm fine."

"You don't seem to be fine."

"Oh... It's just..." Her heart was beating fast and she was struggling to control her breathing. "It's silly."

Erik put his iPad aside and stood up. He was suddenly very interested, watching her intently. "Silly in what way?"

"It's just that... I have this feeling."

"What sort of feeling?"

"It's... like I said it's silly, but..."

"Go ahead. I promise I won't think it's silly."

"It's this feeling that... that somebody's watching me." Mia tried to laugh, but it came out wrong. "That sounds weird, I know."

Erik cocked his head, as if seeing her from another angle would help him to understand. It was a strange move, Mia thought. "Tell me more about it," he said.

"Forget it." Mia shook her head, as if that would shake the odd sensation off. "It's silly. I... I don't even know why I said it. It's probably just moving in and everything."

Erik took a step toward her. The intensity on his face wasn't helping her feel any better. In fact, it was freaking her out.

"What?" She attempted another laugh. "Have I got egg on my face or something?"

He took another step and kept coming until he could take hold of her shoulders and look directly into her eyes.

"What are you doing?" She tried to pull away, but he held her shoulders tightly.

"You should open your eyes," he said.

"What?"

"Open your eyes," he repeated.

"What are you talking about? They are open."

"It's time to wake up."

Mia tried again to pull away, but he just held her tighter. "Let me go," she said, feeling suddenly very weak.

"Wake up."

"What?"

"You should wake up now."

"Why are you saying that? I don't understand!"

"You'll see when you open your eyes." He snapped his fingers in front of her face. "Wake up!"

5.

Ula opened her eyes to find Erik pointing a video camera at her. "Welcome back," he said from behind the lens.

She looked from side to side, trying to get her bearings. With the exception of a single flood light located above the subject chair, where she lay, and a group of blinking lights on the instrument panel, the attic was in total darkness. Ula groaned, then sat up and removed the E.I.R. from her head, being careful not to disturb any of the ninety-two transmitters that were embedded in its padding.

"How long?" she asked.

"Twelve minutes," Erik replied, still recording.

Ula frowned and massaged her temples. "It seemed so much longer."

"You had a sense of time?"

"Yes."

"Does that mean you were able to experience coherent events?"

She closed her eyes and tried to hold onto the images. "Yes," she whispered. "I was there."

Erik lowered the camera. "It was a success?"

Ula nodded. "Yes."

"My god... Ula... This is amazing news. Absolutely amazing!" He raised the camera and pointed it at her again. "Can you describe the experience?"

She took a deep breath. "It... it was like a dream, but... more vivid." She shook her head in disbelief. "It seemed so real. As if I was living it."

"Please look into the camera, Ula. And speak up."

She turned toward the lens, but couldn't bring herself to look straight into it. She spoke haltingly, struggling to capture the details of the memory before it all slipped away. "You were there... in the kitchen... It was that first morning after she moved in. You'd made eggs and... and she came in."

"Yes, that's accurate. What else?"

Ula tried to continue but it was impossible. She turned away and, after a moment, Erik realised that she was crying. "Ula?" He zoomed in on her face. "Why do you cry? Can you explain it?"

She put her hand up to block the camera. "Turn it off."

Erik released the record button and lowered the camera. "Are you crying because you're happy with the success?"

"No..." She needed a moment to gather herself. "It's just... It's just that seeing her again. Being with her. It felt so real. As though... as though she was still alive."

Unsure how to react, Erik put the camera down and pulled up a chair to sit down beside her. They sat there under the flood light for several minutes, neither one saying anything. Then he put his arm around her.

"We've done something remarkable, Ula. Truly remarkable. It's going to have a very big impact."

Uncomfortable with his touch, Ula pulled away and reached for her cane. "That's enough for today," she said, wiping her tears as she headed for the stairs. "We'll continue in the morning."

Leaving Erik to let himself out, Ula disappeared into the safety of her room and lay back on the bed. Closing her eyes, with the sound of cold January rain lashing at the window, she let the emotions of what she'd just experienced wash over her. She had no idea how long she'd been lying there when the doorbell rang.

"I'm sorry to disturb you at this hour."

The woman stood on the doorstep, dripping wet in spite of the small umbrella she held over her head. An attractive thirty-two year-old, she fumbled around in her pockets until she found her identification card, which she displayed for Ula.

"Detective Inspector Sarah Boyd," she said. "We met four months ago, on the night of September twenty-third. The night your housemate -- "

"I know what happened," Ula snapped.

"Of course. I'm sorry. May I come in?"

Ula hesitated, but with no other choice, she stepped aside to let the detective pass. Boyd gave her an embarrassed smile as she closed the rain-soaked umbrella, leaving a puddle on the tile floor.

"Ugly night," she said.

"Yes," Ula confirmed.

"If we could sit down for a few moments... I won't take much of your time."

Ula hung the detective's wet raincoat in the closet under the stairs and led the way into the kitchen, where they sat facing each other across the width of the table. No tea was offered.

Boyd removed a folder from the black briefcase she carried. "I'm sorry to have to revive what must be a very difficult memory, she said. "But I'd like to show you something, if I may."

"All right."

She produced a sheet of paper from inside the folder and placed it on the table. It was a rather crude police drawing of a young man wearing wraparound sunglasses and a black hooded jacket. With so much of his face hidden, the drawing revealed very little about the subject. He was young -- mid-twenties to mid-thirties -- with no facial hair and no distinguishing marks, such as a scar or a tattoo. Aside from that, it could've been almost anyone.

"Is this the killer?" Ula asked.

"He's what we call a person of interest."

"What sort of interest?"

"He was seen in the area on the night of the murder." Ula picked up the drawing and inspected it more closely. It was a photocopy of what looked like a composite, taken from various previously drawn pieces. Like a child's puzzle. "I realise that the hood and sunglasses make it difficult," Boyd said, watching her closely. "But I wonder if it rings any bells for you."

"Should it?"

"Well, as I said to you at the time, I believe it's highly likely that the victim -- "

"Her name is Mia."

"Yes, of course. I'm sorry." Boyd frowned, angry with herself. She knew better than to depersonalise the victim. "I believe that Mia may have known her killer. Does this man look at all familiar to you?"

Ula shook her head. "No."

"A former boyfriend perhaps? Or an unhappy suitor?"

Ula shook her head. "I didn't get involved in Mia's personal life."

"I understand. I just thought that you might've seen someone as they were coming or going. Or that she might've mentioned someone who fits the description."

"No," Ula said. "We never talked about that sort of thing."

"I see. Well..." Boyd stood up. "Thank you for your time. Once again, I'm sorry to have disturbed you."

"May I keep the drawing?" Ula asked.

"Yes, of course," Boyd replied. "Why? Do you feel there might be something you've forgotten?"

"I don't know," Ula said, studying the drawing again. "But it might help me remember." She looked up at Boyd. "I have this problem with my memory."

"Yes." It was in Boyd's notes from the night of the murder. "A bicycle accident, wasn't it?"

"Yes, a bicycle accident," Ula echoed. "Two years ago."

Boyd nodded and offered Ula a business card. "Well, if anything comes back to you, feel free to contact me on this number. Night or day, someone will always answer."

The rain had abated by the time Boyd stepped into the cold January mist. "Well, thank you again," she said as she buttoned her coat.

"Do you think you'll find him?" Ula asked.

"You can rest assured that we'll do everything in our power. No stone will be left unturned."

It sounded to Ula like something straight out of the police training manual. But if they were doing everything in their power, why had it taken four months to put together a bloody drawing? And not a very good one, at that. The detective's visit had done nothing to change her negative opinion of the authorities' competence. They used laughably outdated methods, relying on fallible witnesses to describe dubious memories so that untalented artists could create a useless composite drawing. No wonder an innocent young girl like Mia could be mercilessly stabbed to death less than a hundred yards from her home.

Ula consigned the business card to the top drawer of her bedroom dresser as soon as the detective was gone. She clearly wasn't going to help her find Mia's killer.

But the drawing just might.

6.

It was past nine o'clock by the time Boyd pulled into the driveway of the two-story semi-detached house on Culloden Road. Killing the engine, she took a deep breath and sat there a moment, unloading the day's stress before heading up the path to the front door. Being back in her childhood home still felt a little strange -- sleeping in her old bedroom, seeing all the old neighbours, shopping at all the old shops. She'd returned seven months earlier, shortly after losing her mum to a stroke, in order to look after her father, who'd been diagnosed with early onset Alzheimer's the previous year. It wasn't easy juggling the demands of the job with his care, and there would come a time when it would prove to be impossible, but for now she did her best to appreciate the time they had together.

The only source of light in the house was coming from the television set in the sitting room, where Leonard was ensconced in his favourite armchair, watching an old variety show. In his late sixties, he was a small man, physically fit, with kind eyes and a warm smile. A former detective himself, he'd always been fastidious about his appearance, but more often than not these days, Boyd found him unshaved, in his pyjamas and dressing gown.

"Hello, Dad." She turned one of the floor lamps on.

"Oh, hello, sweetheart." He glanced over. "How was your day?"

"All right, she replied, adding, "The weather's dreadful."

"Is it?" He smiled at her then disappeared back into his programme.

"What are you watching?"

"Oh... Just a bit of nonsense."

She held up a bag of takeaway. "I picked up fish and chips."

"Oh, very nice." His smile turned into a perplexed frown. "Is
it Friday?"

"No, dad. Tuesday."

"Yes, of course it is."

"Shall we eat in front of the telly?"

"Why not?"

Boyd went into the kitchen to prepare the plates and open the
daily beer that she allowed Leonard. Studies had shown that
moderate consumption of alcohol among patients with mild
Alzheimer's could increase their lifespan, so she kept a secret
stash at the back of the fridge, behind the fruit and veggies,
where he wouldn't find it. Not that he was ever a heavy drinker,
but with him being home alone all day, she worried that he
might overdo it without even realising it. She worried about a lot
of things these days.

After dinner in front of the ten o'clock news, Leonard went
up to bed and Boyd retired to the spare room, which she was using as an office, to catch up on paperwork. And there was no
shortage of paperwork. Aside from the witness statements, case
papers, and evidential filings, her mum had left behind a back-
load of unpaid bills, un-filed tax documents, and unresolved
pension issues, along with the numerous other bureaucratic re-
quirements brought about by her sudden demise.

Boyd kicked off her shoes and worked through the various piles until she couldn't take any more. At midnight she checked on Leonard and she was in bed herself a few minutes later. Lying there, waiting for sleep to come, her thoughts turned to the Mia Fraser case. There had been a firestorm of media coverage back in September -- a beautiful young American art student brutally stabbed in Highbury Field for no apparent reason. The case had gone cold until a few days earlier, when a witness came forward. The woman, a neighbour, had said she'd been afraid to get involved at first, and in fact it was her son, a solicitor, who'd eventually contacted the police. A frightened woman with failing eyesight spotting a suspicious-looking character through the window on a dark, rainy night hardly made for the most reliable witness, and the composite itself was of little use. Still, it was all she had at the moment. Perhaps it would be worth putting the drawing out to the media, see if anything useful came back. She resolved to bring it up with the Chief Inspector at the next opportunity.

7.

Ula had been staring at the drawing for over an hour before she finally made up her mind. Returning to the attic, she activated the mainframe, then went to the subject chair and strapped the E.I.R. onto her head. Using the system's dedicated iPad, she dragged the memory folder onto the subject icon, prompting a message to pop up on the screen: *"Send Mia to Ula?"*

Ula confirmed the action, then lay back, closed her eyes, and waited.

"Hey, sweetie. Sorry I'm late."

Kat plopped herself down in the chair opposite and did a quick survey of the cafeteria.

"Meet any hot artists in need of a muse?"

Mia smiled. "Not today."

"Well keep me in mind."

"Of course." Mia pushed a plate across the table. "I got you chicken salad."

"Thanks. So how was the first night in the spook house? Meet any ghosts?"

"Very funny."

Kat shrugged and picked up a fork. "Seriously. How was it?"

"It was fine. Yeah. No problem."

"You don't sound too sure."

"No, it was fine."

"Did she lighten up after I left?"

"I didn't actually see her. She works at night."

"She has a job?"

"She works at home."

"Doing what?"

"I'm not really sure. I met this scientist-type guy this morning. I think he's German."

Kat scrunched up her face. "A German scientist-type guy?"

"Yeah. I think they're doing some kind of experiment up in the attic. They were up there all night."

"Hold on a sec... She works all night in the attic doing experiments with a German-type scientist guy? Okay. I mean, hey... what could possibly go wrong?"

Mia laughed. "Shut up, Kat. It's not like that."

"Sorry, but let's get real. Your housemate is a bit on the weird side."

"You saw her for like two seconds."

"It was enough."

"I don't know. I think she's just painfully shy."

Kat stabbed a piece of chicken. "Well, I guess you're stuck with her now."

"I think it'll be fine once we get to know each other a bit."

"Or you could just avoid her."

"How am I supposed to do that? She lives there."

Kat shrugged. "She doesn't seem like the type that's gonna be easy to make friends with."

"I thought I'd cook dinner for her tonight," Mia said. "You know, a nice bottle of wine to help break the ice."

"Good idea."

"Really?"

Kat nodded. "Sure, why not?" She leaned forward and whispered. "But I'd stay away from that attic."

Mia shook her head. "You're sick, you know that?"

"But in a good way, right?"

"I'm not so sure."

The graphics studio felt stuffy and airless, the toxic smell of the ink overpowering, making it difficult for Mia to concentrate. Slipping out of the afternoon workshop an hour early, she headed east across Granary Square toward the canal, thinking she'd take advantage of the sunny Autumnal day and walk home. The fresh air was already starting to clear her head when she spotted Peter out of the corner of her eye, sitting on one of the stone benches in front of the fountain. In his mid-twenties with a slender build and short bleach blonde hair, he was wearing his usual black leather jacket and, in spite of the cloudy day, sunglasses.

Pretending that she hadn't seen him, Mia adjusted her route, taking the long way around to York Ave. But it was too late. Peter tossed his cigarette aside and was soon walking beside her.

"You blocked me, didn't you?"

She picked up her pace, but so did he.

"Don't ignore me, Mia."

She kept walking.

"I must'a texted you a hundred times," he said but she still didn't respond. "Jesus Christ, Mia! What d'you want me to say?"

"Nothing." She gave him a cursory glance. "I don't want you to say anything."

"So what then? That's supposed to be it? The end?"

"Yes."

"I don't accept that."

"You have no choice."

"Hey, come on, baby. For fuck's sake. Don't be like that." He stepped in front of her, trying to block her way, but she went around him. He caught up again.

"Are you seeing somebody else?"

"That's none of your business."

"Oh, really?" He was quiet for a beat, but Mia could tell he was churning. "Right. Well, I'll tell you something. I really hope you're not seeing someone because if I find out you are, I swear to god I'll -- "

Mia stopped abruptly and swung around to face him.

"It's over, Peter!" Her voice was steady and clear, but her heart was racing. "Do you understand? Finished! And nothing you say or do is gonna change that! So get over it! Move on!"

She slipped past him and walked away as quickly as she could.

"So what d'you want me to do then?" he called after her. "Apologise? Okay then! Jesus Christ, I fucking apologise! I'm sorry!"

Mia didn't look back until she reached Caledonian Road, and then he was nowhere in sight. Okay, she thought, breathing a sigh of relief. Maybe he got the message. She wondered how the hell she ever got involved with a jerk like that. He'd been fun at first, a free spirit who liked to break the rules, and she'd always been drawn to rebels, even back home. But no one had ever hit her before, and one thing was absolutely certain. No one would again.

Not ever.

8.

After a couple of false starts, she gathered her courage, stepped up to the bedroom door, and knocked softly. She could hear movement inside, but it took a moment for Ula to appear behind the crack in the door.

"Hi." Mia smiled nervously. "I hope I'm not disturbing you."

"Is something wrong?"

"No, no, everything's great. It's just that... Well, I was about to cook dinner... this vegetable pasta thing I do. It's not bad, really, and, well, I thought maybe you might wanna, you know, join me."

Ula looked skeptical. "You don't have to do that," she said.

"Do what?"

"Invite me to your dinner. You're allowed to use the kitchen without including me."

"Oh, I know... Thanks. But I just thought... You know, being housemates and everything. It might be nice... I got a bottle of wine. Two in fact. Chianti. I don't know if it's any good, but... anyway. It's up to you."

Ula opened the door a little wider. It was hard not to be taken by the young girl's charm.

"Hey, come on!" Mia smiled. "You can help me chop!"

Ula gave up a little smile of her own. "All right," she said, a little bashfully. As she stepped into the hallway she added a an almost imperceptible, "Thank you."

The kitchen was well stocked with pots, pans, utensils, and everything else you might need, but Ula didn't seem to know where anything was kept. Once they managed to locate a knife and a cutting board, Mia sat her down at the table with a half dozen tomatoes, a couple of courgettes, a red pepper, and a carrot, with instructions to cut them all into bite-sized pieces. Mia sat opposite, doing the onions and garlic.

"You don't need to be so precise," she said, looking at the board where Ula was painstakingly cutting each tomato into eight equally sized cubes, then organising them into a series of absolutely straight lines. "They'll just get squished up in the sauce."

"Sorry." Ula looked down at her work. "I guess I can be a bit obsessive."

Mia pushed the chopped garlic and onion aside. "Why don't I finish that while you open the wine? My pasta always turns out better if I'm a bit drunk."

Ula put the knife down and looked over at the Chianti. "I don't usually drink wine."

"Well, that's not good."

"I'm not even sure I have a corkscrew."

"Then it's a good thing we don't need one!" Mia picked up the bottle and twisted the cap off. "Ta-da!" she exclaimed. "Corks are so old-fashioned, don't you think? However, we will need glasses."

Ula smiled. "Right. I know I have glasses." She retrieved two spotty water glasses from the cupboard and placed them on the table.

"Let the drinking begin!" Mia said as she filled them to the top. "Here's to us. Housemates!"

"Housemates," Ula echoed as they clinked glasses.

9.

"How long was it?"

The voice roused Ula out of her reverie. She looked up from the candle's flame and smiled at Mia, who sat across the dining room table.

"What?"

"You were saying about the coma."

"Was I?"

"Yes."

"What was I saying?"

"You were telling me about the accident."

"Oh..." Ula laughed, a little uncomfortably. "I guess I'm not used to the effect of the wine. It sort of blurs the edges, doesn't it?"

Mia smiled. "That's the idea."

Ula reached out to touch the soft wax at the top of the candle. It felt warm and malleable, pleasant against her fingertips. "I suppose my edges can be quite sharp," she said.

"Not at the moment."

"No," she agreed. "Not at the moment."

The glow of the candlelight on the dining room's rich red walls gave the space a warm, womb-like ambience. Ula couldn't remember the last time she'd been in there, but it felt good, for the moment anyway. Safe.

"So how long were you in the coma?" Mia asked again.

"A little over a year," Ula replied. "Three hundred and nine-ty-two days, to be exact."

"God. It must've been awful."

Ula shrugged. "It was nothing. Like being dead, I suppose. Except that I woke up."

Mia wanted to ask if there had been anyone there for her when she regained consciousness, but it seemed too personal, so she asked instead whether Ula remembered anything about the accident. She shook her head.

"One minute I was on my bicycle and the next I was lying in hospital with a broken body and no memory of what put me there."

"That must've been so frightening."

Mia instinctively reached across the table to touch Ula's arm. It was a simple gesture, expressing nothing more than empathy, but it took Ula by surprise and she recoiled. There was an awkward moment, which Mia used to fill their glasses with the last of the second bottle of wine.

"It's probably just as well that you don't remember," she said. "It would give you nightmares."

"I don't know," Ula mused. "I'd like to remember."

"Maybe you will, you know, with time."

Ula shook her head. "My neocortex was damaged in the accident. It's irreparable."

"Neocortex..." Mia scrunched her face up. "That's like, part of your brain, right?"

"It's where long term memory is stored," Ula replied. "The brain's hard drive."

"So... You have amnesia?"

"It's more specific than that. I have the facts -- name, date of birth, where I went to school -- all of that. But I have no memory of it. No pictures in my head to give it meaning."

"How awful. They just disappeared?"

"No." Ula placed her hand on top of her head. "They're still in there somewhere. I just can't access them."

"No memories." Mia shook her head in a show of sympathy. "I can't imagine what that's like."

"It's like..." Ula paused to consider the best way of putting it. "Like knowing a room full of precious stones is trapped behind a collapsed tunnel, but having no way to get to them."

"How frustrating." Mia sipped the wine. "What do the doctors say?"

Ula waved her hand in the air, dismissing the idea. "They say a lot of things, but they don't know anything. If they can't use a drug or a knife, they're mystified."

"Have you tried therapy? Or hypnosis?"

"Therapy?" A bemused, slightly drunken smile formed on Ula's lips. "I might as well let them attach leeches to my body. It would be just as effective."

"Well, you shouldn't give up," Mia said. "You never know what can happen."

"Oh, I haven't given up," Ula replied, eyes drawn again to the candlelight. "In fact, I'm feeling rather optimistic"

"That's good, Ula," Mia said, reassuring her. "I really do believe that when you're facing adversity, staying positive is half the battle."

Ula was silent, staring into the flame for what seemed a very long time. Then she looked up, smiled cryptically, and said, "Can you keep a secret?"

10.

"Aside from Erik and me, you'll be the first person to see it." Ula led Mia up the attic stairway. "I'm actually quite excited to show you."

"I'm really curious," Mia said, her voice betraying the nervous apprehension she felt.

Ula flicked the light switch at the top of the steps, revealing the makeshift laboratory where she'd spent pretty much every waking hour since coming out of the coma, ten months earlier. Something that looked like a dentist's chair had been set up in the centre of the space, with a computer station behind it. A cable connected the mainframe to a strange looking headpiece that looked like it was made out of a bicycle helmet. Mia stopped a few feet short of the configuration.

"What is it?" she asked.

Ula pointed to the chair. "Sit there and I'll show you."

Mia looked skeptical. "What does it do?"

"If you get in, I'll show you." Ula entered a series of passwords into the keyboard and the mainframe came to life. Mia took a step toward the subject chair but hesitated.

"It's not dangerous," Ula reassured her.

Mia nodded and reluctantly lifted herself into the seat. Ula did something at the control panel and the chair shifted smoothly into the reclining position.

"Just lie back and relax," Ula said, removing a silver clip from Mia's hair before placing the E.I.R. onto her head.

"What's that?" Mia asked, feeling increasingly anxious.

"It's called an Electronic Impulse Receiver," Ula explained. "It picks up electronic signals from your brain and sends them to the computer."

"Oh, wow... Really?"

"It's perfectly safe," Ula assured her as she made some adjustment to the headpiece. "You'll need to close your eyes."

"What's going to happen?"

"You'll see. Close your eyes."

Mia wondered what she'd got herself into. If this was a movie, she was playing the part of the dumb student who was about to be tortured and turned into some kind of zombie by the mad scientist.

"Are your eyes closed?" Ula asked from her seat at the computer station.

"Yes," Mia said as she closed them. "They're closed."

"Good." Ula executed a few quick key strokes on the keyboard.

"Are you relaxed?"

"Not really."

"Nothing bad is going to happen," Ula promised. "But it will work better if you're relaxed."

"I'll try," Mia said, attempting a deep breath but coming up short.

Ula launched the programme software, causing the screen to fill with an erratic pattern of random static noise, similar to an old analogue television when there's no signal. "Now I want you to empty your mind of all thoughts," she said.

"I'm not sure I can do that," Mia responded.

"It's not as hard as it sounds." Ula lowered the room lights from her control panel. "Imagine that you're staring into space. All you can see is a deep, dark, empty void that goes on and on, into infinity. Now allow the emptiness to envelop you... Yes, good."

The electronic noise on the screen slowly diminished, until a calm, almost uniform pattern of black emerged. Ula made a few small changes to the polarity before continuing her instructions in a hushed, flat tone.

"Now I want you to think of a number. Any number between one and ninety-nine. But don't force it. Allow it to come to you. Imagine the number sitting out there in the darkness, a bright white light seared into the empty space. That's it... Now concentrate on it."

As she spoke, something started to form on the screen. Lacking definition at first, it slowly came into focus to reveal the numbers "3" and "7."

"Thirty-seven," Ula said. "You're thinking of number thirty-seven."

"Oh my god!" Mia sat up sharply and twisted around to face Ula, almost pulling the E.I.R. off her head. "How...? How did you...? Did you just read my mind?!"

"I read an image that was in your mind."

"Yes, but... Oh my god, Ula! How?"

"By processing the signal."

"What signal?"

"The electronic signal that your brain transmits."

Mia removed the E.I.R. and looked it over. "This thing can do that?"

"It just picks up the signal." Ula limped over to take custody of the headpiece. "The computer then has to process it. Or more accurately, the software does."

"Amazing!" Mia pulled herself out of the chair. As incredible as the demonstration had been, she wasn't keen on repeating it. Maybe it was some kind of mind trick, she thought. She'd seen that sort of thing on the internet.

"You're a good subject," Ula said as she returned the E.I.R. to its proper place. "You emit a very strong signal."

"Okay, well... I guess that's good. At least I'm unique."

"We each have our own electronic footprint, but you'd be surprised by how similar we all are. As with our DNA, human thoughts are ninety-nine point five percent identical to each other."

Mia shook her head. "I guess all this stuff is beyond me."

"Don't feel bad. It's beyond most people." Ula returned to the control panel to shut the programme down. "Think of the brain as an organic hard drive. It stores electronic impulses and, when called upon, sends them to another part of the brain for processing. Once the signal is intercepted, it's just a matter of teaching the computer how to read it. That's the challenging part."

"So how did you do it?"

"It's like learning a new language. A few years of trial and error, and then all of a sudden, it all makes sense. Once I learned how to send an image to the brain, it wasn't all that complicated to reverse the process. Same language, but instead of talking, I was listening. Downloading, instead of uploading."

"Well, however you do it, it's amazing. But I have to say, it's kind of creepy!"

Ula gave her a look. "Creepy in what way?"

"Sorry..." Mia realised her mistake immediately. She and the wine had managed to lower Ula's guard and now it had suddenly shot up again. "I didn't mean it like that. It's just -- "

"Just what?"

"I guess I don't know why you'd want to read people's minds."

"I don't," Ula said, not bothering to mask her annoyance. "Most of them wouldn't be worth the effort."

"So what is the point?"

"The point is to read my own mind."

"Your own mind? Why would you want to do that?"

Ula gave Mia a long, impatient look. "Because..." she said, drawing it out. "If I can capture my old memories and download them onto the computer's hard drive, I can then reload them into a part of my brain that hasn't been damaged. Isn't it obvious?"

Mia ignored the derisive tone. She was starting to think that rather than some mad evil scientist Ula might be an honest to goodness genius. "Can you really do that?" she asked. "Reload your memories into another part of your brain?"

"There's no reason why not," Ula replied, her irritation dissipating with the question. "I just have to find an access point."

"Access point?"

"A door into my mind. If I can do that -- "

Ula noticed that a strange, distracted expression had come over Mia. She was looking around the attic, as if searching for something in the air.

"Mia...?"

"Yes?"

"What are you doing?"

"Don't you hear it?"

"Hear what?"

"The voice..."

"You hear a voice?"

"Yes. Can't you?"

"No." Ula paused to listen, but there was only silence.

"It's very faint," Mia said. "It's a man's voice, calling out... You really don't hear it?"

"No."

"He's calling out," she whispered. "Calling for you. Saying your name... It's... It's coming from up there..."

She looked up and was met with a sudden blinding flash. Expanding out from its source, the attic was flooded with a light so intensely brilliant that it seemed to burn through everything it touched. Lines blurred and shapes melted into the background, until it finally became impossible to see anything but the white-hot glow of the incandescent haze.

11.

"Ula? ... Can you hear me, Ula?"

Erik held her eyelids open as he flashed the light of a doctor's torch into them.

"Ula!" he repeated. "If you can hear me, you must wake up!"

She was unresponsive, her eyes unfocused and rolling into the back of her head. Erik moved quickly, retrieving the epinephrine injector from the drawer at the computer station, where he'd stored it for an emergency like this.

"Christ, Ula," he whispered to himself as he prepped the needle. "What the hell have you done?"

Concerned that her breathing was shallow and her heart rate becoming dangerously low, he held her head to one side, stabbed her in the nape of the neck, just above the shoulder, and depressed the plunger.

A shiver went through Ula's body, she blinked a few time, then groaned and sat up, holding her head. She stole a look at Erik.

"What happened?" she asked.

"You went online alone."

"Oh..." It started to come back to her. "Yes, I... What... What time is it?"

"It's morning," Erik replied. "Ten past eight."

Ula let out a low moan and massaged her temples.

"You mustn't do that, Ula!" Erik scolded. "You mustn't go online alone! We agreed this. You need to be monitored!" He checked the programme history on the mainframe. "You didn't even collect the data! We must have all the data!"

"Fuck the data!"

Erik was shocked into momentary silence. Ula found her cane, pulled herself out of the chair, and headed for the stairs. Erik followed.

"Did you see something?" he asked.

She didn't answer until they'd reached the bottom of the stairwell. "I'm not sure," she said. "Maybe."

Reaching into her back pocket, she gave him a folded piece of paper. He opened it up to find the police composite of the man in the hood and sunglasses.

"What's this?" he asked.

"A police detective gave it to me."

"A detective? What detective?"

"She came last night. After you left."

"I hope you didn't say anything about our work."

Ula gave him a look of utter contempt.

"It's a reasonable question."

"Of course I didn't say anything."

Erik studied the drawing. "Is he a suspect?"

Ula shook her head. "Someone saw him in the area that night. The detective thinks Mia might have known him."

"So you decided to go looking."

Ula nodded.

"Did you find him?"

Ula took the drawing out of his hand and looked it over. "I don't know," she said, struggling to recall. "There was a man. On a street. He was harassing her."

"Did he look like this?"

"I don't know. Maybe." She closed her eyes and tried to conjure up an image of what she'd seen in the memory. "He... He had blonde hair. Short blonde hair. I think she knew him." An image came to her and she looked up at Erik. "He was wearing sunglasses."

"Are you able to remember anything else about him?"

"No." She shook her head. "That's all."

"A name?"

"A name," Ula repeated. "Yes, there might have been a name."

"Can you remember it?"

Ula stared at the drawing, struggling to recall. But, like a long forgotten dream, the memory was lost, hidden away in some far flung corner of her mind.

12.

Chief Inspector John Baynard looked like he had a case of mild indigestion. But he often looked that way. "For Christ's sake," he moaned as he handed the composite drawing back to Boyd, who'd been waiting by his desk when he came in with his morning coffee. "It looks like half the chavs in London."

"I know it's not ideal, sir, but the witness says she saw him fleeing the scene moments after she heard the victim's screams. I thought that with some media coverage we might get lucky."

"We'd have to get bloody lucky."

Boyd could see it was going be a losing battle, but she wasn't yet ready to sound the retreat. "To be honest, sir, we don't have much more to go on. In fact, we're at a dead end."

"And if we put this out there, the entire world will know it. We'll look desperate."

It was exactly what she'd expected to hear. The case was too high profile to put the drawing out discreetly -- it would be on the front page of every newspaper and featured on every evening news programme, and it would be followed by the inevitable question: *"After four months of investigation, that's all you've got?"*

The truth was that a part of her was relieved. After all, she'd be the one answering the questions. But there really weren't any alternatives. After interviewing all of Mia Fraser's friends, family, teachers, and every resident within two blocks of the crime scene, this was all she had.

"I'm certain we'd get some leads," she said, giving it one last go. Baynard shifted in his seat and cleared his throat a couple of times before answering. It was his way of signalling that he was becoming annoyed.

"Look here, Boyd," he said. "Even if I thought it was worth a punt, I couldn't get it past the crowd upstairs. No one wants to put this back on the front page unless it's because we've got our killer. Show the picture around the neighbourhood, see if you can't get something a bit more solid."

"Yes, sir," Boyd replied, even though she'd already done all that. Returning to her office, she sat at her desk and added the drawing to her file, which contained old news clippings, forensic photos, and a timeline of Mia's movements in the twenty-four hours leading up to her murder. She was a pretty girl, Boyd thought as she contemplated the front page photo in *The Mail*. With the kind of face that made you feel at ease. Non-threatening. Perhaps her assumption was wrong. Perhaps it was just a horrible, random act, perpetrated by a mentally imbalanced stranger. If that was the case, the chances of finding her killer were drastically reduced.

The phone rang. "Boyd," she said absentmindedly.

"Ah, hello, ma'am." The voice was unfamiliar. "This is P.C. Alan Ross, attached to the Edmonton branch."

"Yes?"

"I've got a situation here with a Mister Leonard Boyd. Would that be your father?"

Boyd sat up. "Yes. Leonard Boyd is my father. What's happened?"

"Well, we found him out on the A110, trying to set up a one-man roadblock. He was somewhat confused and, shall we say, inappropriately dressed."

"Oh, god."

"Yes, well, after a cup of tea and a chat he was able to give me your name."

"But he's all right?"

"Yes, ma'am. No harm done."

She breathed a sigh of relief. "Thank you so much for ringing, Officer Ross." She checked her watch. "Are you able to stay there with him for a bit? I'll be as quick as I can."

"Yes, ma'am, no problem."

"Thank you so much. Can I speak to him?"

"I think he'd rather not at the moment." The officer lowered his voice. "I believe he's a bit embarrassed about the situation."

"Right. Yes. I understand." Boyd had her coat on and was already out the door. "Can you text me your exact location?"

It nearly broke her heart to see the expression on Leonard's face as he sat in the back seat of the patrol car. P.C. Ross approached as she neared the vehicle.

"He was a bit disoriented at first," he said. "But he's fine now. Just a bit quiet."

"I appreciate you contacting me."

"Not a problem."

She gave him a nod and approached the patrol car. Leonard, in pyjamas and dressing gown, was drinking tea out of a styro-foam cup.

"Hello, sweetheart," he said, doing his best to put on a brave face.

"Hello, Dad. Shall we go home?"

"Sounds like the thing to do."

Boyd thanked the officer once again and Leonard shook his hand as he got into the car. The short drive home was made in silence.

"Looks like I messed up," Leonard finally said as they turned onto Culloden Road. Boyd looked over at him, but took a moment to formulate a response.

"Do you remember anything about it?" she asked. "How you got there or how it started?"

"No, darling. I'm afraid it's all pretty much a blank."

"Okay," she said as she pulled the car into the drive. "Let's not worry about that now. We'll figure things out."

"Course we will," Leonard said, doing his best to sound convincing.

13.

As Ula slept, Erik returned to the attic, hoping to recover some of the data generated during her unsupervised excursion into the memory file. He was becoming concerned about his partner's state of mind. The emotional stress of the experience was clearly causing her to lose objectivity -- an unacceptable development if the publication of their findings was to be successful. Even with the most diligent methodology and dispassionate presentation, the scientific community would be highly skeptical of the achievement. If a hint of personal feeling was detected, it would be an excuse to reject the entire study, no matter how revolutionary the outcome.

Compounding Erik's unease was the knowledge that he had outlived his usefulness. His expertise had been absolutely essential four months earlier, on the morning after the girl's murder, when Ula first proposed her radical idea. He'd rushed over as soon as he learned of the incident, arriving at half-past seven to find Ula seated at the kitchen table, surrounded by books, furiously making notes on a yellow legal pad.

"It's all over the news," he'd said as he entered, holding up his iPad to display the headlines. "Such a shock. I still can't believe it."

Ula didn't reply, or acknowledge him, so he just stood there, unsure what to do next. "Have you slept?" he finally asked, even though it was clear that she hadn't. There were dark circles around her eyes and she seemed to have been crying.

"No," she responded without looking up.

"Did you eat something?"

She shook her head and again said no. With no food in the kitchen, Erik offered to go out for croissant and coffee, but she wasn't interested, and didn't want a cup of tea, either. So he sat down opposite, taking note of the various volumes she was poring over. Many of them were philosophical in nature -- Descartes, Locke, Dennett -- but there were also volumes by neuroscientists like himself, such as Antonio Damasio and Eric Kandel. He sat silently for several minutes before venturing a question.

"What do the police say?"

Ula stayed focused on her notes. "They say she was stabbed. Eleven times."

Erik winced. "Do they have any ideas?"

She looked up. "Ideas about what?"

"About who is the perpetrator?"

"Of course not. All they can do is ask a lot of stupid questions and hope they stumble on an answer."

Erik nodded. He was unsure how to behave in a situation like this. Ula was clearly upset, but he was sure the last thing she wanted was a shoulder to cry on. She wasn't built that way, and, more to the point, neither was he.

"It was most likely a random psychopath," he said. "It happens quite often in London these days."

She shot him a look, then put her pen down and picked up a book entitled *Broca's Brain.* Erik was familiar with the author, an American scientist named Carl Sagan, but he'd never read any of his works. They'd been popular with the general public in the 1980s.

Opening to a passage that she'd marked, Ula began reading:

"...there is good evidence from modern brain investigations that a given memory is stored redundantly in many different places in the brain. Might it be possible at some future time, when neurophysiology has advanced substantially, to reconstruct the memories or insights of someone long dead?"

She looked up and waited for Erik's reaction. It took him a moment. "Ula... Are you suggesting...?" He paused. "What are you suggesting?"

"You once told me that you captured a signal from a rat that had been dead for two days."

"Yes, it's true, I did that. But -- "

"Then why not a human?"

"Ula..."

"Really. Why not?"

"Why not?" Erik let out a nervous laugh. "Please, Ula. Think what you're saying."

"Is it theoretically possible?"

"Well... Yes. I suppose, in theory it is. But -- "

"If it's possible in theory, it's possible in reality."

He leaned forward. "What *exactly* are you suggesting, Ula?"

She went back to her notes for a brief moment, then put down her pen, sat back, and crossed her arms. "I believe that if we can capture and reconstruct Mia's memory we can use it to discover who killed her."

Erik stared across the table for what seemed like a very long time. "Listen to me, Ula," he finally said. "You're upset and not thinking straight. It's natural, of course, under the circumstances. But what you're proposing is... well, it's... "

"What?"

"First of all, I don't know if it's even possible."

Ula picked up another volume and displayed the title: *The Physiology Of Memory: Beyond Consciousness* by Erik Berg.

"Recognise it?"

"Yes," Erik replied wearily, although he would just as soon have forgotten it. The work had been published several years earlier, to less than universal acclaim. In fact, it had been ignored or dismissed by anyone who mattered.

Ula opened the book and read from the introduction:

"There have been rare, but documented cases in which patients with no active brain functions have regained consciousness. In each of these cases, the patient was able to recount personal memories in full detail. The implication that can be drawn from this phenomenon is that stored memory can survive even when there has been no brain activity for a significant period, which is the accepted definition of death. Put another way, it is reasonable to postulate that a human memory can outlive its host."

Ula glanced up at Erik, then continued reading:

"My own tests have shown that a small mammal, such as a rat, can be frozen to the point of complete organic inactivity, and when thawed out, it is able to regain full functionality. This would seem to confirm that stored memory does not depend on blood flow or other life functions. From these facts, it is reasonable to theorise that quickly cooling a non-active human brain to a temperature low enough to avoid decomposition would preserve the subject's memories, knowledge, and cognitive abilities.

With the proper technology it should be possible, in theory, to retrieve that stored content."

Ula closed the book.

"It's a theory, Ula," Erik said. "Just a theory."

"A theory is a theory until it becomes a fact."

"Yes, of course, but -- "

"Someone is eventually going to do it." Ula picked up her cane and stood up from the table. "You can be the first and go down in scientific history, or you can wait to read about it."

Erik sat back and heaved a sigh. "Even if I could capture a signal, what use would it be? I don't have the capacity to interpret it."

"Yes, that's true," Ula said. "But I do."

14.

The cold storage chambers in the Haringey Public Mortuary maintained a constant temperature of five degrees Celsius -- a sufficient level to delay the decomposition of its unfortunate residents until they found a more permanent resting place. Mia arrived four days after the murder, moved from the police facility by her parents until they could make arrangements for the journey back to Tennessee, where she would be buried in the family plot. Upon learning where she was being held, Ula sent flowers and Erik made arrangements with the night security guard for an after hours visit. No reason was given. Five hundred pounds in cash was explanation enough.

Ula's heart was pounding as they were led into the brightly lit back room. She had insisted on being present for the transfer, but the thought of seeing Mia -- so full of life less than a week earlier -- lying on a cold, metallic slab, filled her with dread.

"You got one hour, mate," the guard said as he slid the drawer open and exited the room. "And not a minute more."

"That will be sufficient." Erik replied, unzipping the black body bag down to Mia's navel. Ula gasped and covered her mouth when she saw the horrific wounds across the poor girl's chest and abdomen.

"You can wait outside if you like," Erik said.

Ula shook her head. "Cover her up," she whispered. "Please cover her!"

Erik zipped the bag back up to Mia's shoulders then placed the small case he'd been carrying onto the stainless steel bed above her head. Reaching into his pocket, he produced a pair of surgical gloves, which he pulled on before opening the case to remove a laptop computer, a small medical drill, and a syringe. Ula felt nauseous as he went to work drilling a half dozen tiny holes into the top of Mia's skull.

"Is that necessary?" she asked.

"I warned you that it would be invasive," he replied, glancing up at her. "Don't worry. It won't take long." He put the drill down and picked up the syringe. "Once I've inserted the implants, the download will take only a few minutes."

"You seem to be enjoying this," Ula said.

"I'm just doing my work."

"That's pretty cold-hearted."

He smiled. "It's not personal for me."

Using the syringe, he inserted a tiny electrode into each of the holes he'd made, placing them on the surface of the brain where they could pick up any signals that were too weak to penetrate the skull. The mini-conductors would then amplify the signal and send it wirelessly to the laptop, where it would be visually registered on a digital storage oscilloscope before it was copied onto the hard drive.

"That's it," Erik announced as he closed the laptop. "There was much more material than I expected to find."

Ula gave him a look. "Are you sure you have everything?"

He displayed a small flash drive which held a backup copy of the file. "It's surprising how little space the contents of a human mind requires," he said. "Thirty-four point seven gigabytes, to be exact."

Ula took the flash drive and grasped it tightly. How strange, she thought, that this tiny circuit board, encased in cheap plastic, contained everything that made Mia who she was. Her memories, thoughts, beliefs, and feelings -- perhaps even her dreams -- all stored in approximately three hundred billion bits of positive and negative electronic charges.

Mia's physical body was dead. Gone forever. But if Ula could unlock the secrets that she held in her hand, she could ensure that her memory would live on forever.

15.

Wiping the steam off the clouded bathroom mirror, Mia stopped short upon seeing her own face looking back at her.

There was a gap. Clearly she'd just stepped out of the shower, but she had no memory of it. Or getting out of bed for that matter. Had she been sleepwalking? She tried to reconstruct the events leading up to that moment, but they were gone, out of reach. She recalled having dinner with Ula the previous night, but it seemed distant, unfocused. Like a long forgotten dream. Feeling a cold shiver, she wrapped a towel around her naked body and shut her eyes. But the darkness was unsettling, frightening even.

By the time she'd dried her hair, done her make-up, and got dressed, she was feeling herself again. Late for class, she sprinted down the stairs and headed for the door.

"Good morning."

"Oh..." Mia spun around to find Ula standing in the kitchen doorway. It felt like she'd been lurking. "You startled me!"

"I made coffee."

"Oh, right." She forced a smile. "Thanks, but I'm really late. I've got class..."

"You should eat something before you go. I saw some eggs in the kitchen. And some bread. It's a bit stale but we could do French Toast. Or whatever you like. I don't mind."

"If I wasn't so late, I'd really love that." Mia pointed toward the door. "But I really am late. I'll, um... I'll see you later, okay?"

"Yes. All right. We can talk later."

It sounded ominous, but Mia didn't want to be drawn in. "Okay," she said as she opened the door. "Have a good day!"

"What time will you be home?"

"I really don't know, Ula." She made an effort not to sound annoyed, but it was pretty obvious. "It kind of depends, you know."

"I see. Well. I suppose it can wait. Since you're in such a hurry."

Mia sighed and shut the door. "What can wait? Is there a problem?"

"No..." Ula took a step closer. "Well, I don't know really. It's just that I... I don't really remember very much about last night. The wine... it left me a bit, well... unclear." She took another step closer and lowered her voice. "Did anything unusual happen?"

"How do you mean?"

"I... I found this in the attic." She held her hand out to display Mia's silver hair clip. "It's yours, isn't it?"

"Yes." Mia took the clip. "I guess I must've left it up there."

"We went up there?"

"Don't you remember?"

"No, I... As I said, the wine affected me."

"Oh, right." Mia eyed the door. She really wanted to escape, but Ula clearly had something more to say.

"Did we go into the attic so I could show you the image processor?"

"Yes! And it was amazing! Like you were reading my mind!"

Mia had forgotten about it herself until that moment. Maybe the wine had affected her, too, she thought, although she didn't recall it ever having that effect in the past.

"I really shouldn't have showed you," Ula said. "It would be a problem if Erik knew."

"Listen, Ula, you don't have to worry about that." She reached out and touched her arm. "It can be our secret. You and me, okay?"

Ula smiled. "Yes, okay. I like that. Our secret."

"Good. But I really do have to go now. I'm so late!" She headed for the door. "I'll see you tonight, okay? You can try to explain to me how you do it!"

"Yes, all right," Ula replied. "Tonight."

As Mia stepped onto the pavement, she had that feeling of being watched again. Glancing back at the house, she half expected to find Ula watching her. But the door was shut, the curtains drawn.

16.

It wasn't bad, she thought. One of her better efforts, in fact. But something was bothering her. Taking a few steps back, she tilted her head to one side and squinted, trying to see it from another angle. It was a bigger canvas than she'd ever attempted and she was starting to think that she'd been a bit too ambitious.

"It's good."

Thinking she was alone in the studio, the voice from behind startled her. Spinning around, she came face to face with the life model who was the subject of her painting.

"Oh," she said. "Thanks. Do you really think so or are you just saying that to be nice?"

"Honestly?"

"Yeah. Honestly."

"All right then. Honestly..." He crossed his arms and contemplated the painting for quite a long time. "I think it's good," he finally said. "*Very* good."

"Really?"

"Yes, really. Although..."

"What?"

"I think you've made me better looking than I really am."

Mia smiled and avoided the trap. "Yeah, well, you know. Artistic licence."

The model laughed. Tall, muscular, and darkly Mediterranean with wavy black hair and a thick, rather dreamy accent, he was clearly well aware of his exceptional good looks. He looked even better in the creamy white silk dressing gown that was wrapped around his torso.

"I'm Nico," he said, letting his robe fall open as he offered his hand. Considering that she'd just spent several hours studying his naked form, it shouldn't have been embarrassing, but it was. Somehow, being half exposed was more suggestive than full on nudity.

"Mia." She responded with a sheepish smile as she accepted his hand.

"Is it finished?" Nico asked, turning back to the painting.

"I'm not sure." Mia started cleaning her palette. "I'll have to see how I feel tomorrow."

"Are you always so cautious?"

She gave him a look and smiled. "I'm gonna have to think about that one."

He laughed again and reached into his pocket. "Well, while you're thinking, a friend of mine is throwing a big party tonight. You should come."

Mia looked down at the flyer he was holding out:

!!! EVICTION PARTY !!!
Help Us "REDECORATE" Our Loft
Live Music | Live Art | Open Bar
Iak

"It's gonna be crazy," Nico said.

"Yeah?" Mia took the flyer. "What kind of crazy?"

"The wild kind."

He winked at her, which should've come off as laughable, but somehow it worked. "The address is on the back," he called out as he headed for the changing room.

"Can I bring a friend?" Mia called back.

"Of course!" He glanced over his shoulder. "As long as she's as sexy as you!"

Mia shook her head and turned back to the painting. He was right, she thought. It was good. The composition, the colour, her brushwork... it had all come together in a very pleasing way. Still. Something about it was disturbing. Something that gave her a knot in the pit of her stomach.

She had no idea why.

17.

Kat pulled the Mini into an empty space on the Crescent, switched the engine off, and turned to Mia. "Is she gonna be there?"

"She usually is," Mia replied as she stepped out onto the pavement.

Kat made a face and followed her up the walk toward the front entrance. "I just hope she doesn't give me that evil eye treatment again. It's creepy."

"She'll probably be up in the attic," Mia replied. "She practically lives up there."

"Lives in the attic. Okay. Nothing to worry about there."

Mia gave her a 'knock it off' look and Kat shrugged.

"What's up there, anyway?"

"The torture chamber, of course!"

"Ha ha, funny. But I wouldn't be at all surprised."

Mia laughed and slipped the key into the front door. The house was quiet, as usual, and the girls maintained a wary silence as they slinked upstairs into Mia's room and closed the door. The plan was to get ready in Highbury, grab a bite on Upper Street, then take an Uber to the party.

Mia was unsure at first if she was up for it, but Kat's enthusiasm had swept her along. "How often do we get invited to a party in Shoreditch?" she'd said. "Never, that's how often!" Still,

Mia couldn't quite shake a niggling apprehension about the evening. Nothing definitive or overwhelming. Just a vague sense of foreboding that she did her best to ignore as they dressed and did their makeup.

"So who invited us?" Kat asked as she added the final touches to her face.

"This model guy," Mia replied. "I've been doing a painting of him."

Kat gave her a look. "Oh, yeah? Like a portrait?"

"No, it's for life class."

"So... he's naked?"

"Nude," Mia corrected her.

Kat raised an eyebrow and went back to her mascara. "And...?"

"And... what?"

"And... You know what."

"I don't know. Depends on your taste I guess."

Kat gave her a look. "So you expect me to believe that you've been staring at this completely naked man for hour after hour, and you haven't thought about whether he's hot or not?"

"Okay, he's hot."

"I knew it!" She added a touch of gloss to her scarlet lips. "You think he'll have a friend for me?"

"It's not a date, Kat. It's a party."

"If you say so." Kat made a final check in the mirror. "But I'm warning you, whatever happens, I'm so not going home alone tonight."

Mia laughed, doing her best to ignore the knot that was tightening in the pit of her stomach.

"I didn't hear you come in."

Ula emerged from the dining room, intercepting the girls as they headed for the door.

"Oh, Ula. Hi." Mia faked a smile. "We just... We didn't want to disturb you."

"Oh." Ula shot Kat an unhappy look. "I see."

"We thought you might be, you know, working."

"No." She looked them up and down, from one to the other. "You look all dressed up."

"Yeah, well... There's this, um, party... A friend from school... We, you know... We thought we might as well check it out."

"Oh. That's nice. I hope you enjoy it."

Ula stood there, expressionless, for an awkward moment, leaning on her cane. Mia thought she was about to say something else, but she just turned away and silently retreated back into the dining room.

"Let's go," Kat whispered, edging toward the door.

"I better talk to her," Mia replied, pulling her arm out of Kat's grip. "She's obviously upset about something."

Kat frowned and waited by the door as Mia went into the dining room. She found Ula standing at the table, placing several containers of takeaway Chinese back into the bag they'd come in. An open bottle of wine and a lighted candle sat in the middle of the table.

"You didn't tell me you had plans," Ula said. "In fact, you said we'd talk tonight. At least, that's what I remember. But perhaps I've got it wrong."

"I'm so sorry, Ula -- "

"I can't cook, so I got takeaway."

"I totally forgot..."

"I'll put it in the fridge. You might be hungry after the party. Or shall I just throw it away?"

"You have every right to be angry. I -- "

"What makes you think I'm angry? I just assumed that when you said that we'd talk tonight, you meant it."

"I... I feel awful, Ula." Mia took a step toward her. "Listen... Why don't you come with us to the party? It might be fun."

Ula shot her a bitter smile and glanced down at her cane. "I'm not much of a party person."

"Right. Well..."

Mia wasn't sure what she could do or say to make things better, so she just stood there. After what seemed like a very long time, Ula sighed, looked up, and offered what seemed like a genuine, if a little sad smile.

"Don't worry," she said. "I'll get over it."

18.

Kat looked back across the park toward the house and shook her head. "I don't care what you say, there's something seriously wrong with that woman."

"She had an accident." Mia glanced over her shoulder, as well, and wondered if Ula was watching them. "It was pretty serious."

"Yeah? What happened?"

"A bus hit her while she was on her bike."

"Well that accounts for the cane, but not the weirdness."

"She was in a coma for like a year." Mia felt suddenly and inexplicably agitated talking about it. "I think it really messed her up."

"Messed her up how?"

"Memory problems, for one. Kind of like amnesia, but not exactly."

"So she has brain damage?"

She shot Kat a look. "I wouldn't put it like that. She's incredibly smart. Maybe even a genius."

"A genius with brain damage. Hey. What could possibly go wrong?"

Mia came to a sudden stop and turned sharply on her friend. "To tell you the truth, Kat, I've really had about enough of your bitchy comments about her! She's actually a very nice person who just happens to be a little screwed up!"

"Hey..." Kat raised her arms in a defensive posture. "Sorry. I didn't know you two were so tight."

Mia frowned, a little surprised at the intensity of her own reaction. "We're not. It's just... I don't know... I don't even know why I said that. I... I guess I just feel sorry for her."

"Hey..." Kat could see that Mia was upset. She ran a hand along her arm in a soothing motion. "I get it. I'll shut up about her, okay?"

"Okay. Yes. Thanks."

They walked on in silence for a few moments, then Kat turned and gently asked, "Are you all right, sweetie? Because you seem a bit -- "

"What?"

"I don't know," Kat searched for the right word. "A bit off."

"Do I?" Mia forced a smile. "Oh. Well... It's nothing a large gin and tonic won't cure."

"Amen to that!" Kat said, returning the smile.

Mia did her best over drinks at the local pub to hide the increasing sense of angst that had taken hold of her. Something wasn't right, she knew that, but it was elusive, impossible to grasp let alone identify or confront. It felt as though some corrupting virus had found its way into her system and taken control, leaving her to watch in helpless anticipation as her life moved inexorably toward some impending disaster.

She felt it. Something bad was coming. Something sinister and dangerous. But there were no forks in the road, no off ramps, no choices that would allow her to avoid the catastrophe. How could there be? Mia didn't know it, of course -- not yet -- but the truth was that her future had already happened.

By the time they hit Shoreditch it was dark and Mia was feeling more relaxed. She was also feeling the effects of three G&Ts as they climbed a set of steep narrow stairs to enter the third floor loft. The place was huge, a former warehouse with painted brick walls, high ceilings, and a raised gallery with a glass balustrade along the far end. The music was deafening, the lights flashing, and the space jammed with people, mostly young and alternative, or trying hard to be.

"This is what I call a party!" Kat yelled above the noise.

"Crazy!" Mia shouted back.

A dude in a paisley shirt and flowers in his hair emerged from the crowd and pointed a Polaroid camera at them. "No, no, no, darlings! Don't pose!" He gestured wildly with his free hand. "Reveal yourselves! Show me your greatest desires and your deepest fears!"

Kat gave him the finger and Mia stuck her tongue out.

"Perfect!" The photographer cooed as he snapped the shot. "You see how the camera reveals the truth!" He displayed the faded, unfocused shot that the camera spit out.

"Can we have it?" Kat asked.

"Are you serious?" He shot her a look and stuffed the snap-shot into his pocket. "Find your own fucking truth!"

"Asshole!"

But he was gone, swept away by a heaving vortex of dancing humanity. Kat laughed and shouted into Mia's ear, "Fuck the truth! Let's find the bar!"

"I see it over there!" Mia yelled back. "Follow me!"

Squeezing through the crush, Mia became aware that some-where along the way, she'd lost Kat. Looking back, she saw her being pulled onto the dance floor by a blonde Rastafarian with a silver waistcoat, a gold nose ring, and a live monkey on his shoulder. The last thing she saw of her friend that night, she was dancing with the Rasta man, the primate firmly attached to her head.

"I have no idea what I'm doing here."

Mia hadn't noticed the frail-looking young man in khaki chinos and a black polo neck, but he'd been watching her from a distance for quite a while before gathering the courage to walk over, lean into her ear, and deliver his line. He looked young -- sixteen or seventeen -- and a bit lost, but having been on her own since being abandoned by Kat, Mia was relieved to have someone to talk to.

"What's anybody doing here?" she replied.

"Exactly!" the boy exclaimed. "What's anybody doing here? I mean, it's all so pointless, isn't it?"

Mia took a sip of the drink she'd picked up along the way. It seemed like vodka, but she wasn't sure. "You are talking about the party, right?"

"What?"

She raised her voice. "When you said you have no idea what you're doing here, you meant the party, right? Or did you mean life in general?"

"Which is the better answer?"

Mia laughed. "Neither one is an answer! They're both questions!"

"I'm confused!"

"Aren't we all!"

"Is that a question?"

"No, it's a statement!"

"Oh." The boy shrugged and reached into his chinos. "You wanna smoke some dope?"

Mia hadn't been stoned more than a couple of times since leaving Franklin High, and not at all since arriving in London, but this seemed like a good moment for it.

"Why not?" she shrugged.

The boy smiled. "Is that a question?"

"Yes, but a rhetorical one!" Mia stole the joint out of his hand and put it between her lips. "Which means you don't have to answer!"

Things got a little strange from there. Maybe the weed was stronger than Mia was used to, or maybe it was laced with something, but whatever the reason, the boy started to make even less sense than he had when she was only drunk. Half his words sounded like gobblygook and the other half weren't much better.

"Have you ever wondered if we actually exist?" he said in all seriousness.

"No," Mia replied. "Why would I?"

"Did you know that our physical bodies are made up of ninety-nine point nine percent empty space?"

"Speak for yourself," Mia shot back, holding her breath as she took another drag off the joint.

"Hey, who knows? Maybe we're just some alien being's crazy daydream. Or a giant hologram projected onto some distant galaxy."

Mia exploded into laughter.

"What? What's so funny?"

She wasn't sure if he was offended, indignant, or baffled, but it didn't matter. Whatever the case, the expression on his face was maybe the most hilarious thing she'd ever seen. She couldn't stop laughing.

"You know that's an actual theory in Quantum Physics, right? It's called the Holographic principle and it's supposed to explain black holes. Hey...! Where you going...? Are you coming back?!"

The boy's voice faded away and the next thing Mia knew she was sitting on a toilet with her head in her hands. Realizing that she hadn't pulled her jeans down, she checked her crotch and was relieved to discover that it was dry. The sounds of the party helped her recall where she was, but she had no memory of how she'd ended up in her current position. Grabbing hold of the sink, she pulled herself up onto her feet and looked into the mirror. Someone had written a message in lipstick across the glass, asking the question:

"What the fuck are you looking at?"

Stepping out of the bathroom, Mia found herself on the raised platform overlooking the dance floor, which seemed to have grown even more frenzied since she last saw it. The floor was pounding, or maybe it was her head. An unpleasant wave of disorientation came over her, making her feel that she was watching herself from some place very far away. She needed to get out, to be alone and breathe some fresh air. Spotting the stairs, she pushed past a group on their way up, then forced her way through the crowd, heading for the exit. As she was about to escape, someone grabbed her arm and pulled her back in.

"Hey! Where you going?!"

It took a moment for his face to come into focus, and even then Mia wasn't sure she could trust what she was seeing.

"Peter? What...? What are you doing here?"

"Some fucking insane party, right?!"

Mia looked down at her arm, which he held tightly. "Can you let go of me, please?" she heard herself saying.

"You can't leave now!" His smile looked crazed, menacing. "Things are just heating up!"

She tugged at her arm but couldn't get free. "Let go of my arm!" she repeated. "You're hurting me!"

"What?"

"You're hurting me!"

"Can't hear you!"

"Have you been following me?"

"We need to talk!"

"I don't want to talk!"

An ominous look came over him and he tightened his grip. "For fuck's sake, Mia! How long are you gonna keep this bull-shit up!"

"You're hurting me!"

"You made your point and I said I'm sorry! So let's just for-get anything ever happened! We'll start over, fresh!"

"I don't want to start over! Now let me go!" She knew the look in his eye. He was going into one of his rages.

"Jesus Fucking Christ!" he howled. "You're acting like a goddamned spoilt little bitch! And I swear to god, Mia, if you're fucking somebody else, I'll fucking kill you both! And you know I ain't just saying it!"

Mia tried again to wriggle out of his grasp, but he was too strong. Her arm was starting to go numb.

"GO AWAY!" she cried.

His response was to yank her toward the door, so hard that it felt like her arm would come out of its socket. After dragging her a few steps he stopped abruptly in front of the exit, which was blocked by Nico, the model. Peter tried to pull Mia around, but Nico blocked him again.

"You got a problem, mate?" Peter said, puffing his chest out.

"It don't look like she wanna go with you," the bigger man replied.

"Yeah, well, it's got fuck all to do with you." Peter tried to push his way through, but Nico shoved him back, nearly knocking him off his feet.

"You need to let go of her arm," Nico said, stepping forward. "Right away."

"Or what?" Peter responded, holding his ground.

Nico shrugged. "I fuck you up."

Peter stood there a minute, an inane grin plastered across his face, but after the pitiful show of defiance, he released his grip on Mia. "Fine," he said. "Take her. She's ain't worth the trouble anyway."

"Go to hell!" Mia cried out as he headed for the door.

"Oh, yeah? Well, we ain't done yet!" He pointed a threatening finger in her direction. "Don't you worry about that! We ain't anywhere near done!"

19.

Staring out the window at the dark, windblown streets, Mia was grateful that Nico had offered to drive her home, but she was even more grateful that he didn't feel the need to fill the space with meaningless small talk. Whether it was the after effects of the drug or the traumatic events of the evening, she was in a delicate state and the silence was welcome.

Her thoughts drifted back to the funny kid in the chinos and black polo neck. He seemed like a nice boy in spite of his weirdness and she regretted being so rude to him. She wondered if he found a more sympathetic ear for his crazy ideas after she so abruptly abandoned him. She hoped so. And who knows. Maybe his ideas weren't so crazy after all. Maybe everybody really was just playing a role in some alien's daydream. Sometimes things felt that way.

"We arrive."

Nico finally spoke up as he pulled the car onto Highbury Crescent. He parked in front of the house, turned the engine off, and killed the lights.

"Thanks," Mia said, reaching for the door. "Thanks for everything."

"It's no problem." He gave her a sympathetic smile. "And you? You're okay now?"

"Yes, fine, thanks." She responded with her own tentative smile. "Just really tired. I'll see you in class, okay? Thanks again." She started to open the door but Nico reached across to pull it shut.

"Why don't you stay for a minute?" he said. "We can talk a little."

"Thanks, but -- "

"But what?" His arm was draped across Mia's lap, his face too close to hers. The sweetness of his cologne made her feel vaguely nauseous.

"Let's talk at school, okay? I really should go in now."

Nico withdrew his arm, but remained uncomfortably close. "Tell me something," he said. "This asshole who makes trouble. He's been your boyfriend?"

"I guess so, more or less. But not for very long."

Nico frowned. "You shouldn't go with a man like this. He's not good for you."

"Yeah, well, it's over now."

"Good. You definitely need something better."

"Look, Nico, I'm sorry, but I'm really not up for talking right now. I appreciate everything you did, but, like I said, I'm pretty exhausted -- "

He moved a little closer. "Do you?"

"Do I what?"

"Appreciate what I did."

"Yes... Of course I do, but -- "

"Then why don't you show it to me?"

A shot of adrenaline surged through Mia's body and her heart started to pound wildly. "Show you what?"

"Show me the appreciation."

"Hey, I don't know what you thought but -- "

Before she could finish the sentence, he reached over, grabbed her hand, and pulled it onto his hard cock, which he'd somehow managed to slip out of his trousers. Mia yanked her hand away.

"Jesus Christ! What's wrong with you!"

"Hey, don't worry... You gonna like it, I'm sure." He tried to grab her hand again, but Mia shoved him away.

"Asshole!"

She fumbled for the door handle but Nico grabbed her by the collar, pulled her back, and, laughing, tried to kiss her. Acting on pure instinct, Mia clenched her fist and brought it around hard, landing a direct hit on the side of his face. It took a beat for the blow to register, then he exploded in anger.

"FUCKING BITCH!"

He reared back and delivered a brutal backhand, his pinkie ring cutting a deep gash above her eye. As blood spilled out from the wound, she went for the door again, but he dragged her back in. Grabbing her by the scruff of the neck, he pushed Mia's head down into his lap and thrust his pelvis up into her face.

"You wanna make it like this?" he snarled. "Okay! We make it like this!"

Surging with adrenaline and bleeding badly, Mia flailed about, desperately searching for something, anything to help her escape the brutal assault.

The persistent blare of the car's horn lifted Ula out of a semi-conscious state. Opening her eyes, she lay there a moment, mind not yet fully engaged, unable to process the disturbance outside her window. Then, suddenly, she sat up.

Grabbing her cane and pulling on her dressing gown, she stumbled down the stairs and out the door. As she stepped into the cool night air the honking abruptly stopped, and so did Ula. She could see movement inside the car -- two people struggling -- but it was too dark and she was too far away to make out any detail. Heart pounding, she moved cautiously down the steps and walked toward the vehicle.

When the car door opened, Ula froze. An image of what would come next flashed through her mind -- the blood, the tears, and the harrowing events that would inevitably follow -- and the thought immobilised her. Unable to take another step into that horrific future, she just stood there, paralysed, eyes shut tightly.

"Ula?"

The lighthearted tone of Mia's voice and the playful laugh that followed was enough to prompt Ula to open her eyes. She found the young girl standing a few feet away, looking a bit drunk, but happy and unharmed.

"What are you doing out here?" she asked, unable to hide her amusement at the sight of Ula standing there in her nightshirt and dressing gown. "You know you don't have any shoes on, right?"

Ula shook her head, searching for a rational response. "I was in bed and... and I heard something. There was a noise."

"A noise?" Mia reached into the black cab that had brought her home and paid the driver.

"Yes. A car... It kept honking and it woke me up."

Mia collected her change and the taxi drove off. "It must have been an alarm," she said.

Ula frowned. "Something is wrong," she said.

"Well, you'll catch cold standing there like that." Mia headed up the path toward the house, but stopped halfway when Ula didn't follow. "Ula? Aren't you coming in?"

"I... I don't think I can."

"What do you mean you can't? Why not?"

"I'm stuck."

"Stuck?"

"Yes, I... I can't seem to move."

Mia took a few steps back toward Ula. "Well, it's your own fault, isn't it?" she said.

"My fault?"

"Of course it is!"

Ula frowned. "I... I don't understand."

Mia sighed in frustration. "Well, you see, you're in control now, so you can do whatever you want. If you can't move it's because you don't want to."

"I do want to," Ula said, a hint of panic creeping into her voice. "But I can't seem to go forward and I can't go back."

Mia shrugged. "Maybe you should just leave then."

"Leave?"

"Yes. Leave."

"How can I leave when I'm stuck?"

"Drink the water," Mia replied.

"The water?"

"Yes."

"What water?"

"Just drink it, Ula." Mia's voice was suddenly mixed with Erik's.

"Go ahead," they said in unison. "Drink."

20.

The sensation of the cold, wet liquid against her lips was enough to pull Ula out of the dream. She allowed a few drops to seep into her mouth before opening her eyes.

"Welcome back," Erik said.

Ula pushed his hand away, spilling the water across her chest, then she pulled herself up into a sitting position. Feeling dizzy and vaguely nauseous, she removed the E.I.R. from her head and looked around the attic in an attempt to get her bearings.

"There was quite a bit of brain activity," Erik said as he returned to the computer station to check the data. "And you were in almost constant REM. How much do you remember?" He picked up his camera but put it back down when Ula gave him a look.

"How long this time?" she asked, rubbing her temples.

"I woke you after thirty minutes. I'm afraid that a longer period would make it too difficult for you to make a complete account of the memory."

Ula frowned. "What day is it?"

"Saturday."

"Day or night?"

"Morning. A few minutes past eleven o'clock."

Ula bowed her head and closed her eyes, which only made her feel more lightheaded. "I don't remember starting the session," she said.

"Interesting." Erik made a note in the logbook. "But perhaps not so surprising. Your brain has quite a lot to process at the moment. More important is what you're able to recall from the experience."

Ula located her cane and dismounted from the subject chair. "I don't want to talk about it," she said as she headed toward the stairway.

"But you must talk about it... Ula? Where are you going?"

"I'm not feeling well," she replied as she disappeared down the steps. "I'm going to lie down."

Erik sat back and took a deep breath. Ula's emotional reaction to the memories was becoming increasingly troublesome. If she was now going to refuse to share her experiences, the study would be doomed, which simply wasn't an option. This was a once in a lifetime opportunity and he wasn't about to let it slip away.

Following Ula downstairs, he tapped several times on her bedroom door before getting a response. "Go away," she finally said.

"All right," he replied. "I'll do that. But I want you to know that if I leave now, I'll not be coming back." He waited for an answer, but there was none, so he continued. "And Ula... you should know also that I will be taking the memory files with me. The original and the backup copy. I feel this is justified since I was the one who -- "

The door opened and Ula appeared. "You can't do that," she said, fixing him with a steely gaze.

Erik returned her look for a brief moment, then he turned and walked away. "It's quite a nice day outside," he said without looking back. "Perhaps some fresh air will be useful to our discussion."

The caf was filled with cliques of young mothers and their loud children taking a break from the playground so, in spite of the January chill, Ula chose an outside table. Erik went in to order and came back with two steaming cups of tea.

"Strong with no sugar," he said as he sat down. "Unlike me, who takes two. What can I say? I have a sweet tooth."

Ula saw through his attempt at small talk and had no patience for it. "You can't take the files," she said.

"I don't see why not," he replied. "After all, I was the one who extracted them."

"They'll be useless without my software."

"Precisely." He stirred his tea. "Separately, we have nothing. But if we can find an acceptable way to work together, we will have created something truly revolutionary. Imagine, Ula, the applications a process like this will have. I truly feel that we have a unique opportunity to make an important contribution to science, and even to mankind."

"And here I thought you just wanted to win the Nobel Prize off the back of my work."

An acidic smile formed on Erik's lips. "Whether we like it or not, we find ourselves in a codependent relationship. You can choose, of course, to end it. But if you take that option, I will stand up right now and walk away. With the files."

Ula sat there for a moment, perfectly still, staring into her teacup. "What do you want?" she said without looking up. Erik took his phone out of his pocket, opened the audio recording application, and placed it on the table between them.

"Everything," he said. "All that you can remember."

Ula turned away and gazed out across the open space of the park. Somewhere in the distance, a dog barked at an unseen disturbance. When she finally spoke, it was in a whisper.

"She was raped."

The word stunned Erik into silence. "I'm sorry," he said after a moment. "It's terrible that you had to see this."

"I didn't see it," she replied bitterly. "I experienced it."

Erik nodded. "Yes, I understand." He furrowed his brow and leaned forward. "What can you recall about this incident?"

Ula sighed, then closed her eyes and lowered her head into her hands. "We were in a car," she began slowly. "He'd driven me home... from a party. Yes. That's right. There was a party. Crowds of people and loud music. And drugs... I smoked something..."

"*Mia* smoked something."

"Yes." Ula acknowledged. "Mia smoked something."

"And what happened in the car?"

"She tried to get out, but he wouldn't let her."

"Can you describe this man?"

"No..." She closed her eyes, trying to conjure up the memory. "It's too dark. I can't see his face."

"A name? Can you recall his name?"

"No, I -- "

"Do you believe this man was the killer?"

"I don't know."

"Did he possess a knife?"

"I don't know," Ula repeated, more forcefully.

"How did the episode end?"

"I don't know!"

"Was this the night she was -- "

"I DON'T KNOW!"

Ula pounded the table, drawing the attention of two young mothers who were leaving the café. They exchanged a look and quickly herded their young ones away, whispering as they went. Erik waited until they were in full retreat before turning back to Ula.

"You must try to remember what happened next."

"I don't have to try. I know what happened."

Erik frowned. "I don't understand. If you know what happened next, why is it that you don't know how the assault concluded?"

"Because it changed."

"Changed?"

"Yes."

"What changed?"

"The memory."

"In what way did it change?"

"I was there, inside Mia -- in her head -- when she was attacked. But then..."

"Yes?"

"It all changed. Suddenly, I was in my bed... and I was me again."

"You were Ula?"

"Yes."

"What happened then?"

"There was a noise... a car horn. It woke me up. I knew something was wrong. I sensed, somehow, that Mia was in trouble so I rushed outside. But when I got there, it was all different. She was getting out of a taxi and... she was fine. Everything was fine. It was as if the attack had never happened."

Erik sat back in his chair, folded his hands together, and observed Ula for a moment. "Do I understand it correctly that you saw two entirely different memories?"

"Yes."

"And they were in direct opposition to each other?"

"Yes."

He thought about it for another moment. "Which one is correct?"

"I don't know."

"But you were there, weren't you? At the original event."

"Yes."

"So you must know which scenario actually happened."

She shook her head. "They both happened."

"Of course, I understand. In your mind they both happened. But in reality, only one memory can be correct."

"I don't know. I suppose so."

"It's not a supposition, Ula. It's a fact. There is only one reality and if you don't realise this, well then -- "

"Then what?" She looked up sharply.

"Then we have a significant problem."

She fixed him with a long, cold stare then picked up her cane and stood up. "I don't remember what happened," she snapped. "And to be honest, I don't give a fuck."

"Yes, I can see that," Erik replied, but she was already walking away. He sat there a beat, then sighed and got up to follow.

"Would you like to know what I think?" he said when he'd caught up.

"Not really."

"I think you enjoy being together with her again and you would prefer to stay there, in the past. But your subconscious knows how badly it ends, so it has decided to change the memory in order to create a more satisfying outcome. I believe your personal feelings are corrupting her memory."

Ula shot him a sideways glance. "Go to hell."

Erik shrugged. "It's not surprising, really. To alter history by changing the memory of it is a natural human trait. But this time, instead of altering your own memory, you are altering hers."

Ula turned to face him. "What's your point?"

"I believe we need to make a change in the protocol."

"What sort of change?"

"Your emotional involvement is making it impossible to gather accurate data. Therefore I suggest that, when we resume the study on Monday morning, you will take my position at the control panel and I will take over as host to the memories."

"And if I don't agree?"

"I'm sorry, Ula, but in that case I will have no choice but to withdraw from the study. And you will lose forever the memory of Mia."

21.

Watching the steady drip, drip, drip of the leaky tap put Ula into a trance-like state. Upon returning to the house she'd quickly stripped off and slipped into a steaming hot bath, hoping it might wash away the bitter aftertaste of Erik's vile betrayal. The thought of him roaming around in Mia's memory, intruding on her secrets -- *their* secrets -- made her feel physically ill.

Closing her eyes, she allowed herself to drift into deeper waters. It was a familiar place, a sanctuary where she could escape the hard edges of the physical world without disturbing the demons that lurked in the dark depths of her unconscious mind. Here, she could be truly alone, and in control.

Ula had always sought out solitude. Even before the accident she'd lived a life of almost complete anonymity, striving to avoid the clumsy awkwardness of social interaction whenever possible. It wasn't that she didn't like people, it was more that she feared them. More specifically, she feared the way they made her feel when it became clear -- which it did almost immediately -- that she had no idea how to act with them. It was as though they all knew the script by heart while she had no idea what her lines were supposed to be. Most of the time it didn't matter as she found most people predictable and tedious, but even when she found someone of interest -- a fellow student or, later, a colleague or co-worker -- something prevented her from being able to connect in the way that others could.

It got worse after the accident. Unwilling to take up her position back at the institute, or to share her findings with its directors, her funding quickly disappeared. She continued her work, alone in the attic, using her trust fund money until it ran out, at which point she had no choice but to write a grant proposal. The initial interest it generated swiftly vanished when Ula failed to appear at the personal interview -- she'd rehearsed the meeting for weeks and even dressed for the occasion, but when it came down to it, she couldn't bring herself to leave the house.

She fell into a deep depression. The more she slept -- which was most of the day -- the more exhausted she felt. And the more exhausted she felt, the more she slept. With curtains drawn and no outside contact, time became a meaningless concept and Ula had no idea how many days or weeks had passed when the bell rang and she found a tall, slightly awkward German intellectual standing on her doorstep. Erik had introduced himself and explained that he'd seen her proposal and would be willing to finance the study himself if she would agree to take him on as a partner. The fact that he didn't bother with small talk and made no effort to ingratiate himself gave Ula the confidence to accept his proposal. That and the knowledge that she had no alternatives.

It was at Erik's insistence that she advertised for a lodger. While he was happy to subsidise the study, he wasn't willing to support Ula herself, no matter how meagre her needs were. And, he argued, it was a terrible waste to have such a big house filled with empty rooms. She put the idea off for as long as she could, but Erik finally placed the ad himself.

Mia had awakened something in Ula. Though blissfully unaware of the effect she was having, the young girl touched a place that had never before been reached by another human being. Perhaps, after a lifetime of emotional exile, Ula needed only the most basic offer of friendship to construct the misguided idea that some deep bond existed between them. Or maybe she simply fell in love, as happens every day. In the end, it didn't matter. Whatever the truth, losing Mia had been a devastating blow, and not a day had gone by since the murder that she hadn't thought about joining her in death. Whatever that might be, it had to be better than the purgatory she existed in now.

"Then do it!"

The voice startled Ula out of her reverie. She shot up out of the water into a sitting position, wrapping her arms around her upper body to cover her nakedness. But looking around the darkened bathroom, she saw that she was alone.

22.

The Met Police tactical unit pulled into Strathan Close at precisely 5:30 AM and came to a stop in front of the target property. The two bedroom council house had been under surveillance for several days following a tip from a neighbour that there was an unusual amount of comings and goings at the premises. When it became clear that many of the comers and goers were known street dealers, a warrant was obtained and the early morning raid was put into effect.

A half-dozen officers, dressed in protective body armour, emerged from the vehicle and moved quietly into position, two men proceeding to the rear exit while the remaining four prepared for a frontal assault. On a signal from the sergeant in charge, the lead man stepped forward and, with one powerful blow from a battering ram, shattered the early morning calm.

In the upstairs front bedroom, Peter leapt out of bed and pulled his trousers on as the girl from the pub -- he forgot her name -- sat up and started screaming. Grabbing his trainers as the intruders barrelled up the narrow staircase, he was halfway out the window before the officers dragged him back in, held him face down on the carpet, placed him in handcuffs, and escorted him down to the kitchen.

The sergeant in charge greeted him with a smile. "Have a seat." he said.

"I ain't sayin' nothing," Peter hissed as he was guided into a chair.

"No need to. I'll do the talking, at least for now."

The sergeant removed a driving licence from the wallet he was holding.

"Peter Greene..." He looked up and smiled again. "I'm arresting you on suspicion of the illegal distribution of a controlled substance. You do not have to say anything, but it may harm your defence if you do not mention when questioned something which you later rely on in court. Anything you do say may be given in evidence. Do you understand?"

"Fuck you," Peter mumbled.

"I'll take that as a yes."

"Take it however you want."

"Right. So, then, tell me, Peter..." He looked through the cupboard and drawers as he spoke. "How long have you resided at this address?"

"I didn't say I do, did I?"

"Don't you?"

"I don't have to say nothin'."

"How about the girl?"

"What about her?"

"She live here or just visiting?"

"None of your business."

The sergeant was about to respond when one of his men stepped into the room. "I think you'd better see this," he said, holding out a Nike shoe box. "Found it in the closet, hidden under a pile of dirty pants."

The officer placed the box on the table and removed the lid, revealing a collection of newspaper clippings. Picking out the top article, he unfolded the front page of *The Sun,* dated 24 September, and displayed it for the sergeant. Above a photo of Mia, smiling and happy, the headline screamed in big, bold ink:

"TOO YOUNG TO DIE!"

23.

Boyd didn't hear the phone ringing until she stepped out of the shower. Slipping into her dressing gown, she noted that it was a blocked number and picked up.

"Boyd," she said, rubbing her hair down with a hand towel.

"Ah, good morning, Detective..." It was an unfamiliar voice but she could tell right away that he was a cop. "This is D.I. John Nichols at Wandsworth station. Sorry to ring so early on a Sunday, but I've got a customer down here that I think you might want to have a chat with."

"Oh?" Boyd perked up. "In what regard?"

"In regard to Mia Fraser."

The bedside clock read 8:27 AM. "I can be there by ten," she said.

"Great," Nichols replied. "I'll meet you at the detention centre. Know where you're going?"

Boyd said that she did and they ended the call. After quickly dressing she found Leonard in front of his bedroom mirror, in a crisp white shirt and grey slacks, struggling to get his tie right. "Damn thing keeps coming up short," he grumbled, hand shaking as he pulled the knot apart and lined it up again.

"You don't have to wear a tie if you don't want to, Dad."

"Well, I want to."

"Let me help you then." She took a step into the room but his look stopped her in mid-step.

"I can still tie me own tie, thank you very much. I'll be out shortly."

The trip to the Hounslow hospice, where Leonard's older brother, Trevor, was in care, had been planned since the previous weekend, when Boyd learned from her cousin Alice that time was short. The brothers, who were eight year apart, had never been especially close -- they hadn't seen each other in years -- but Trevor was Leonard's only surviving sibling and Boyd understood how important the visit was to her father.

"We'll have to make a stop in Wandsworth," she said when he finally appeared in the sitting room, his tie the perfect length.

"What's in Wandsworth?"

"I have to see someone. It won't take long and it's more or less on the way."

Leonard managed a weak smile. "All right, sweetheart."

After a couple of attempts at small talk, Boyd got the message that her father preferred to be left alone with his thoughts, so they drove most of the journey in silence. It gave her time to wonder who Wandsworth had in custody and what light he or she might be able to shed on the Mia Fraser murder. A new lead would certainly be timely. The composite drawing had gone nowhere and, with nothing else to pursue, the case was in danger of slipping into cold storage.

Nichols was sitting in the otherwise empty lobby of the detention centre, eyes closed, listening to music on his earbuds. It was obvious from the jeans, old jumper, and blue gilet he was wearing that it wasn't a work day for him, either.

Boyd leaned over and poked his arm. "Detective Nichols?"

He opened his eyes, pulled the buds out, and produced a slightly embarrassed smile as he stood up. "Ahh... hello. You must be -- "

"Sarah Boyd." She offered her hand.

"John Nichols," he reciprocated. In his mid-thirties, with curly black hair, he had a pleasant, honest face. Boyd absent-mindedly checked her watch.

"I hope I haven't kept you waiting too long."

"No, no, not a problem. Just got here myself." He smiled again and glanced over at Leonard, who'd stopped at the door to look at the postings on a bulletin board.

"Oh, that's my father," Boyd explained. "We've got a family thing after this, so..."

"Got it," Nichols said. "He okay to wait out here?"

"Yes, of course," she said, then called out. "Dad!"

He looked over and smiled.

"This is Detective Inspector John Nichols. He's going to take me inside to interview his prisoner."

Leonard stepped up and offered his hand. "Detective Chief Inspector Leonard Boyd," he announced, then added with a wink, "Retired."

"Good to meet you, sir." They shared a firm handshake. "Like father, like daughter, eh?"

"Taught her everything she knows."

"I'll bet you did."

"Right, so..." Boyd stepped in. "Dad, you'll have to stay out here while Detective Nichols and I go inside. There are some magazines on the table, why don't you choose one and I'll be back as quickly as I can."

"Sure." Leonard gave her a peeved look. "You do what you have to do. Don't worry about me." He stood there until Boyd and Nichols had disappeared through the security door, then he picked up an out of date copy of *The Radio Times,* sat down, and turned to a random page.

"Nice man, your dad," Nichols commented as they walked a long grey corridor lined with blue steel doors.

"Thank you. Yes, he is."

"Where was he based?"

"Enfield was his last posting," Boyd said. "He took early retirement a couple of years ago."

"I understand," Nichols said and Boyd gave him a look.

"Do you?"

He nodded. "I went through it with my mum. It's not easy."

"No, it's not."

They reached the end of the corridor and stopped in front of a door marked 'Interrogation Room.'

"Right!" Nichols opened the case folder he'd been carrying and read from the arrest report. "Peter Alan Greene. Twenty-six years old, no fixed address. A few minor arrests, all drug related, with the exception of a GBH a couple of years ago. No convictions, but several cautions."

"What's the connection to Mia Fraser?"

"He was picked up in a raid on a drug distribution house in East Putney early this morning." He handed her a plastic sleeve that contained the collection of news clippings that had been found in Peter's closet. "He seems to have a special interest in your case."

Boyd could see that certain passages had been underlined. "Has he been interviewed?" she asked.

Nichols shook his head. "I thought you'd want first crack."

"Thank you," she said as they entered. "I do."

Peter was seated in the small, windowless room, head bowed, hands folded together on the table. He looked up when Boyd and Nichols entered, but said nothing.

"Good morning."

Boyd took the seat opposite and conspicuously turned on the recording equipment. Nichols remained standing, leaning against a wall near the door.

"I'm Detective Inspector Sarah Boyd and I'm going to be asking you a few questions," she began. "Also present is Detective Inspector John Nichols. You should know, Mister Greene, that this interview is being recorded and in the event that you are charged with a crime, you will be given access to a copy of the recording. Do you understand?"

He was silent. Boyd waited to establish eye contact before she repeated the question.

"Do you understand what I said, Mister Greene?"

"Yeah, I understand."

"Good. Thank you." She opened the file on the table in a way that allowed him to see the plastic sleeve holding the clippings. "Now, if you could, Mister Greene, please explain how you knew Mia Fraser."

No response. Just an icy stare.

"Did you have a personal relationship with her?"

Still nothing.

"Had you ever been intimate with her?"

Peter looked away and faked a laugh.

"Had you ever spoken to her?"

"I got nothing to say to you," he mumbled.

"I see." Boyd turned to Nichols. "You know what I think?"

"What?"

"I think he fancied her and she told him to piss off."

Nichols looked Peter up and down. "Yes, that makes sense. I mean, why would a beautiful young girl like that have any interest in a born loser like him? Yeah. I think you've got it. She rejected him so he killed her. I'd put money on it."

"Fuck you, mate." Peter shifted uncomfortably in his seat.

"I think we struck a nerve," Boyd said.

Peter shook his head. "What a joke!"

"Really?" Boyd leaned forward. "You find the killing of an innocent young girl laughable, do you?"

Peter reverted to silence.

"All right," Boyd continued. "Let's start at the beginning. Where did you first come into contact with Mia Fraser?"

"I didn't say I ever did, did I?"

"You might as well tell us because it will be very easy for us to establish whether or not you knew her. It would be far better for you if we got that information from you."

He gave her a long look. "I didn't kill her."

"Well, you certainly seem to have had a special interest in the gory details. Personally, I'd call it a rather sick interest." She picked up the plastic sleeve and read from the top clipping: "'...the nineteen year-old art student suffered multiple stab wounds and was pronounced dead at the scene.' Why did you underline that bit, Peter? The bit about 'multiple stab wounds.'"

"Last I heard there's no law against reading a newspaper."

"Did it turn you on?"

Peter looked away and Nichols spoke up again.

"I'll bet he liked to take them out at night and read them over and over. It would have helped him to re-live the experience. To go over it, moment by moment."

"Is that right, Peter?" Boyd tried to establish eye contact again, but this time he avoided her look. "You clearly enjoyed reading about it. Was it to help you to re-live the experience, like Detective Nichols said?"

"That's ridiculous," Peter scoffed.

Boyd could see that he was becoming agitated. "All right," she said. "Let's just go with the facts. Such as, where were you on the night of September twenty-third last year?"

Peter sat back in his chair, gave her a nasty look, then turned to Nichols.

"I want a lawyer," he said.

24.

Reaching into the darkness, Ula located her phone on the bedside table and swiped her finger across the front panel, bringing the screen to life. 6:53 AM. She'd slept badly, lying awake for hours before finally drifting off, only to be roused by yet another troubled dream that slipped out of her grasp as soon as she re-entered consciousness.

Rolling onto her back, she slid a hand into her panties and allowed herself a moment of pleasure. It was a rare indulgence, and she always felt ashamed afterward, but it provided relief from the increasing angst that gripped her, day and night, over the past few weeks. The comfort was fleeting, of course, and only served to make her feel a little more empty inside, a little more alone.

She slipped out of bed, picked up her cane, and limped into the bathroom to wash her hands. Alone for most of her life, Ula had never felt lonely until she lost Mia. It was difficult to say what had been different about the young artist, but from the moment she turned up on the doorstep, with that beautiful, open smile and the soft, friendly southern American accent, Ula had been won over. She'd always dismissed the idea of 'love' as an embarrassing fabrication created by song writers and novelists, but if such a thing as heartbreak existed, this was it.

There was no food in the kitchen, at least nothing worth eating, and Ula had no appetite anyway. Filling the kettle, she stared out the rain-splattered back window and cast her mind back to the night, four months earlier, when she and Mia sat in that very room, drinking wine as they prepared their one and only meal together. Strange, she thought, to have seen that evening through Mia's eyes, and how different the young girl's experience had been from her own. She hadn't been aware of Ula's heart pounding with excitement as they spoke, or her hands trembling as she tried to cut the vegetables for the sauce, and Mia had no idea about the shiver that went up Ula's spine when her new housemate reached across the table and touched her arm. Perhaps she should have confessed her feelings, but there was so little time.

Carrying her tea into the sitting room, Ula was drawn to the piano. She hadn't played in longer than she could remember, but something made her take a seat on the bench and open the fall-board. After sitting there for several minutes, eyes closed, her hands moved, in a seemingly involuntary movement, onto the keys. The notes came effortlessly, some deeply rooted memory guiding her fingers; some new, unfamiliar emotion inspiring a flawlessly tender performance of Beethoven's *Moonlight Sonata*.

Of all the mysteries in life, 'falling in love' might be the most bewildering. Why and when it happens is as inexplicable as why the vibrations from a particular group of tightly wound steel strings, when organised in a certain way, can make a human cry. But, in the end, the how and why of losing your heart to another doesn't really matter. For whatever reason, Mia became the receptacle for all the years of Ula's unspent affections and then, as suddenly as she was found, she was lost.

Ula dried her tears and curled up on the sofa under the woollen blanket she'd had since childhood. Erik was a selfish bastard, she thought, and one way or another she would have to prevent him from taking over Mia's memory. But he was right in his analysis. She no longer cared about revealing the murderer's identity. In fact, now that she knew what it was to see through Mia's eyes, it was the last thing she wanted to experience. She just wanted to go back there, to recapture the past and yes, even to change it. Was there anything wrong with that? Given the opportunity, wouldn't any one of us accept a second chance?

Daylight was fading when she was roused by the sound of the doorbell. Sitting up slowly, she reached for her cane, but it wasn't where it should have been. Disoriented and not yet fully awake, she surveyed the room and saw that it had been left on the piano, laid out across the keyboard. Strange, she thought. Why would she have left it there? And how?

The bell went again, more persistent this time. Dragging herself off the sofa, Ula crossed the room to retrieve the walking stick, then made her way to the entrance hall and opened the door. She remembered the detective's face but not her name.

"I'm sorry to disturb you again, Ms. Mishkin, but if it's convenient I'd very much appreciate a few moments of your time." Met with a vacant stare, and aware of Ula's memory issues, Boyd started over. "Sorry," she said. "I'm Detective Inspector Sarah Boyd. I was here a few days ago with -- "

"The drawing. Yes, I remember."

"That's right." Boyd smiled, but it seemed disingenuous to Ula. "It would be very helpful if I could have a few minutes of your time."

"Does it have to be now?"

"If you don't mind."

Ula hesitated, then nodded and stepped aside.

"Thank you," Boyd said as she crossed the threshold. "I promise it won't take long."

Ula was suddenly aware that she was still in her pyjamas and dressing gown. "I... I should get dressed," she said.

"Yes, of course." Boyd replied, smiling again. "Take your time. I'll wait here."

As Ula disappeared up the stairs, Boyd edged away from the door to have a look around. There was a strange, somewhat unsettling energy in the house -- a sense that something, or someone was lurking around the corner. A less rational person might have attributed the unexplained undercurrent to a ghostly presence, but Boyd dismissed all that otherworldly nonsense. She was simply curious.

Stepping into the sitting room, she gravitated to the same group of photographs, sitting atop the piano, that Mia had come across on her first night in the house. The smallest photo, in black and white, showed a young woman standing outside an institutional-looking building in a wide open, rural setting. In her mid-twenties and wearing a white lab coat, the woman's pose was noticeably stiff, showing only a trace of a smile on her thin lips. The year, 1974, was scrawled in the lower righthand corner of the picture, along with a few words written in Russian. The second photograph, in faded colour, featured the same woman, but this time she was standing in front of the house on Highbury Crescent, clutching a pram that held identical twins. Bundled up in matching hats and coats in spite of the springlike weather, the two infants stared out at the photographer with the same solemn expression their mother exhibited. The third and final photograph depicted the woman, perhaps a bit older, standing with a group of men in front of a chalkboard that held a long mathematical equation. Unlike the men, who seemed happy and collegial, the woman stood apart and gazed off into the distance, as if completely unaware of her surroundings.

Boyd replaced the photos back onto the piano and moved to the bookshelves, which were filled with an eclectic mix of old art books, hardcover copies of classical musical compositions, and a large number of thick volumes of works in physics and biology. Noticing what looked like an old journal wedged between the paintings of Marc Chagall and a treatise on thermodynamics by German physicist Max Planck, Boyd pulled it off the shelf and turned to the first faded page. The author had inscribed her name at the top -- *Olga Mishkin* -- along with the date of the journal's initial entry, which was *01.01.1970*. Below that was a two paragraph entry, written in Russian, which included a couple of mathematical formulas and, at the bottom of the page, a small pencil sketch of a sleeping cat.

Leafing through the remainder of the diary, Boyd found that the writings became increasingly erratic. The words no longer fell in a straight lines across the page, letters were exaggerated in size or printed backwards, and the drawings became progressively sinister, with an assortment of monsters and demons replacing the sleeping cats and flowers of the earlier pages. In the last few entries, entire passages were crossed out and on the final page, dated *10.10.1996*, the words had been so thoroughly scratched out with black ink that the paper had started to tear.

"Why are you looking at that?"

Boyd spun around to find Ula standing behind her. "Oh..." She closed the journal. "Sorry, I was just admiring the collection..."

Ula stepped forward, took the book out of Boyd's hand, and replaced it on the shelf. "I live alone so I'm not used to locking the doors." She turned away and limped toward the hallway.

"I do apologise," Boyd said, following her out of the room. "I had no business -- "

"Did you want to ask me something?" Ula interrupted as she shut the sitting room door behind them.

"Yes... Yes, I did." Boyd reached into her coat pocket and handed Ula a photograph. "I wondered if you recognise this man."

Ula drew a sharp breath. "Peter," she whispered.

"You know him?"

"No, I... I don't think so. No, I don't."

"But you know his name."

"Yes, I... I just remembered it. When I saw the picture."

"Sorry," Boyd said. "I'm a bit confused. You don't know him, but you recognised his picture right away and you know his name."

Ula couldn't stop looking at the photograph. "He did it," she said after a long pause. "He killed her."

"Why do you say that?"

"Because he said he would."

"This man threatened Mia?"

"Yes."

"He said he would kill her?"

"Yes."

"Did you witness him making that threat?"

"Yes..." She paused and finally looked up from the photo. "I mean no."

Boyd frowned. "Which is it?"

"I... No. I wasn't there."

"Then how do you know he threatened her? Did Mia tell you about it?"

"Yes." Ula handed the photo back. "In a way."

"In a way?"

"Yes."

"You're going to have to be more specific."

Ula nodded. "I'll try, but... Have I told you about the problems I have with my memory?"

"Yes, I understand about that. But it's very important that you give me a clear and honest account of everything you know about Mia and this man, and how you know it. I'm happy to take your statement here, or if you prefer, we can do it in a more official setting, at the station."

It was a clumsy threat, but it worked, as Boyd knew it would. Feeling that she needed time to organise her thoughts, Ula suggested they sit at the kitchen table with a cup of tea.

"Did Mia have a relationship with this man, Peter Greene?" Boyd activated the voice recorder on her phone as Ula sat down.

"Yes," Ula replied. "But it was over. She'd ended it before she came to live here."

"And he was upset about that?"

Ula nodded. "He followed her everywhere. He'd wait outside the art college and say things to intimidate her."

"Was that where he threatened to kill her?"

Ula thought for a moment. "No. That was at a party. There were lots of people there, and it was very noisy. I tried to leave but he grabbed me by the wrist and wouldn't let go."

"Grabbed *you*?"

"I meant Mia. He grabbed Mia."

"And that's when he threatened to kill her?"

"Yes."

"Do you know what exactly he said?"

Ula closed her eyes to help her recall the moment. "He said, 'If you're fucking somebody else, I'll fucking kill you both.'"

"I see. And you know this in such detail because..."

"Mia told me."

Boyd noticed a slight hesitation in Ula's response. "Did Peter Greene ever appear at this property?"

"No," Ula replied. "He never came here. I would have known about it if he did."

Boyd paused. Something wasn't right and she needed a moment to consider the best approach. "The problem I'm having, Ula..." she began after a moment. "...is that the last time we spoke, you told me that you never discussed Mia's personal life with her. Now you say that she confided to you all the intimate details of her failed relationship. Why didn't you tell me about this threat when we first spoke, four months ago?"

Ula frowned and allowed herself a sip of tea. "I sometimes have trouble remembering," she said. "As a result of my injury."

"Yes, I appreciate that," Boyd replied. "And it's a reasonable explanation for why you might've forgotten your conversation with Mia. But there's another point that's not so easily explained."

"Yes?"

"If you weren't present when Peter confronted Mia outside the college, or at the party, and you're certain that he never came to the house, how is it that you recognised his photo?"

Ula had no satisfactory answer. She couldn't tell the truth, of course, and Boyd wouldn't have believed her even if she did. In the end, she mumbled something about Mia showing her a picture on her phone, but Boyd knew a blatant lie when she heard one.

25.

The streets were jammed with Sunday evening traffic heading back into the capital so it was after seven by the time Boyd pulled into the drive. She'd tried calling Leonard several times along the way, but kept getting the *'Please Try Again Later'* message. His phone had likely run out of battery, as was often the case, but it was still a concern.

She'd spent most of the journey thinking through her conversation with Ula. None of the information she provided could be used to make the case -- even if it wasn't hearsay, you could hardly find a worse witness than someone who keeps telling you they suffer from memory loss. But while her account was confused, and even a bit strange, Ula had established in Boyd's mind that Mia and Peter Greene had been involved in a romantic relationship, and that when she dumped him he stalked her and threatened her life. A crime of passion certainly fit the particulars of the attack, and this wouldn't be the first time a woman died because a man couldn't handle rejection. But she would need some pretty conclusive evidence to charge him with the murder. Or a confession.

She found Leonard in the kitchen, carving up a roast chicken. "Hello sweetheart!" He turned and gave her a broad grin as she entered. "Perfect timing. I thought I'd do us a chicken. I hope you're hungry."

"Now that you mention it, I'm absolutely starving."

"Good. I've got roasties and cauliflower cheese in the oven. I can't guarantee the gravy, but I've had a go at it."

"Wow... You did this all yourself?"

"Oh, well, now you've caught me out. The truth is I've got bloody Jamie Oliver tied up in the back room. Of course I did it myself! I'm not totally incapable, you know. Not yet!"

"I know that, I just... I don't remember you ever cooking, that's all. It was always mum."

"Well, everybody's gotta start somewhere. So why don't you get us each a lager from that secret hiding place you've got under the carrots and then set the table. We'll eat in the dining room for a change."

"All right then," Boyd said, pretty close to speechless. "Two lagers coming up."

It had been ages since they'd used the dining room, which was usually reserved for visitors, and they'd stopped coming months ago. The normal routine was to sit in front of the telly with a takeaway or a ready meal and watch the news or some nonsensical game show until they were both too tired to keep their eyes open. It was a pleasant change to see the good plates and cutlery out on the table, and to have the comforting scent of a Sunday roast fill the house.

Whatever had passed between the two brothers at the hospice, it seemed to have taken a great weight off Leonard's mind. He was more relaxed and engaged than Boyd had seen him a very long time. She had hung back, in the outer room, chatting with cousin Alice while Leonard sat at his older brother's bedside, holding his hand as he slipped in and out of consciousness. Boyd knew there were issues between the two men that had gone unresolved for many years, but her sense was that it had all melted away without having to be directly addressed. Just being there, and perhaps sharing a memory or two, was enough to make things right.

"Have you ever seen a Sunday roast as pretty as that?" Leonard stood back from the table and admired his work.

"Let's hope it tastes as good as it looks," Boyd replied with a smile.

"Well, let's dig in and find out!"

The conversation continued to focus on how wonderful the meal was for several minutes, and that led into memories of Sunday dinners past, which were always preceded by a long walk in Trent Park.

"Do you remember the time we lost Roxie?" Boyd asked, referring to the black Dachshund who was a constant companion for the first ten years of her life.

"Oh, yes, I do," Leonard replied even though he didn't. "She wasn't the sharpest tool in the box, was she?"

"She was sweet."

"Right. Sweet and thick as a brick."

Boyd smiled at the memory. "I remember when I asked how you knew where to find her, you said you had to think like a dog."

"Is that what I said? Think like a dog?"

"I had no idea what it meant."

He chuckled. "I suppose it means follow your nose."

"Well, I was very impressed. And grateful."

Leonard paused, then reached over and put his hand over his daughter's hand. "Listen, sweetheart," he said. "I want to talk to you about something."

Boyd suddenly understood what the dinner was all about. It was a conversation she dreaded, but she'd known for some time that it was coming. "All right, Dad," she said. "You have me well primed. But you know how I feel."

"Yes, I know how you feel, darling. But we have to face facts. There's going to come a time..."

"That may be, but we're not there yet."

Leonard sat back in his chair and frowned. "I'm afraid we might be getting pretty close. And, you know, the last thing I ever wanted to be is a burden."

"You're not a burden, Dad. I think you proved that today."

"Listen, sweetheart. You have to get on with your own life. How are you going to do that while you're stuck here looking after me?"

"Dad -- "

He raised his hand to stop her. "Now listen," he said in his father voice. "It's not all about me being noble and unselfish, either. I have a certain amount of pride -- as you well know -- and I don't particularly like being treated like a five year-old by my own daughter."

"Dad, I try not to -- "

"I'm not saying I don't deserve to be treated like a five year-old. I'm saying I don't like it."

Boyd leaned forward, folded her hands onto the table, and gave her father a look. "Okay, now you listen to me, Dad. You're not going anywhere. We're both going to stay right here and make this work, just as we have been for the past seven months. If it gets to the point where I can't handle it, I promise that I'll let you know, but until then, that's the plan. Okay?"

Leonard gave her a gentle smile, nodded his head, and said, "Okay. For now, anyway."

That settled, they returned to a discussion on how good the dinner was. Boyd volunteered for clean up duty, but Leonard insisted on giving her a hand. As she finished scrubbing out the last pot and gave it to him for drying, she ventured a question that she'd wanted to ask for some time, but hadn't had the nerve.

"Can you tell me what it's like, Dad?"

"What what's like, sweetheart?"

"Your episodes. I mean, do you feel them coming on, or... I don't know. Perhaps it's too difficult to describe."

Leonard thought about it for a moment. "Well..." He tilted his head and looked up at the ceiling as he thought about it. "It's not as though I'm aware of anything happening. And it seems to come out of the blue, without any warning whatsoever. At least none I'm aware of. I could be feeling quite clear and sharp -- as I am right now -- and then... How to explain it? I suppose it's a bit like going into a tunnel, but without knowing you're in it. And the tunnel keeps getting more and more narrow, until it finally goes totally dark and..."

He frowned, struggling to find the words. Boyd wished she hadn't put him on the spot like that.

"You lose yourself," he finally continued. "Perhaps that's the best way to describe it. You lose yourself. Does that make any sense?"

"Yes... Yes, it does. Thank you."

"I wish I could explain it better."

"No, you did well."

"Good." He winked and his expression went from serious to suddenly mischievous. "How about I ask you a question now?"

"Okay," she replied cautiously. "Go on."

"What did you think of that detective chap this morning?"

Boyd hadn't known what to expect, but it certainly wasn't that. "Detective Nichols?"

"That's the one."

She laughed. "I don't know what to think of him. I don't know him."

Leonard shrugged. "He seemed like a nice chap. And he's a cop. You two would have a lot in common."

"All right, Dad. That's enough."

"I'm just saying, that's all. I mean, you know, sweetheart, you have to keep an eye out. You're not getting any younger. And I could tell he liked you by the way he -- "

"Leave it, Dad, before you dig that hole any deeper."

Leonard shrugged and Boyd flicked the kettle on. "I'm going to have a cup of tea. Would you like one?"

"No, darling, that's me done. I'm off to bed." He gave her a peck on the cheek. "Don't stay up too late."

"Goodnight, Dad."

Boyd decided to make it an early night, as well. She checked the doors, carried her tea up to bed, and was soon in a deep, comforting sleep, taking one of those long Sunday walks in the park. The world was so detailed, so vivid and real, that she had to wonder how she had ever come to believe that mum and Roxie were gone forever.

26.

It was absolutely ridiculous to feel awkward, she knew that, but Leonard's comments the previous evening made Boyd hesitate for a beat before dialling. Yes, Detective Nichols seemed like a nice man, and he certainly wasn't hard to look at, but she never would've considered him in that light if her father hadn't said what he said. It was a bit annoying.

"Ah, Boyd..." Nichols picked up on the first ring. "I was just about to call you."

"Oh?"

"Yes. Our man seems to have secured himself a duty solicitor. So if you want another go at him, you've got the all clear."

"I would, yes. As soon as possible."

"Right. I'll get on to counsel and get you a time."

"Great. Thank you."

"No problem. I'll give you a buzz."

"I'll wait to hear from you."

Boyd put the phone down, shook her head, and frowned as she checked her email. It had been over a year since things petered out with the paramedic, but she was quite happy with the way things stood at the moment. Between her case load and looking after Leonard there was no room for anything else, not now and not in the foreseeable future. She was getting on just fine without a man, in spite of what Leonard thought, so she would just have to put those thoughts out of her mind and get on with the tasks at hand.

No response from Baynard yet. She'd sent the Chief Inspector a message on the departmental system about an hour earlier, detailing the developments in Mia's case. She didn't expect anything other than the usual "follow up and don't screw up" reply, and she would've preferred to wait until there was something a bit more conclusive to report, but it was wise to keep the C.I. in the loop. He always seemed to find out anyway.

Retrieving the case file, which she kept locked in the bottom drawer of her desk, she opened to the top sheet. Skimming over the basic facts -- nineteen years old at the time of her death, 168 cm in height, hazel eyes, dark brown hair (dyed blonde), one small tattoo of a red rose on her left ankle, and no discernible scars -- she skipped ahead to the transcripts of various statements taken from friends, neighbours, and family until she found the one she was looking for.

Katherine Anne Ellis. The interview had been taken by a colleague, but Boyd remembered that the girl -- who went by the nickname "Kat" -- had become extremely distressed when she was informed of her friend's fate. Boyd also recalled, although her memory was a bit vague, that when she was interviewed on the day after the murder, she'd indicated that Mia had recently split up with a boyfriend. Locating the relevant exchange in the transcript, she read the following:

Question: *Did Mia ever discuss with you, or are you aware of, any intimate relationships she was currently involved in?*

Response: *No, she wasn't seeing anyone. Not that I know about anyway, and she would've told me if she was.*

Question: *Are you aware of any relationships that she might have been involved with in the recent past? One that might have ended recently?*

Response: *No, not really.*

Question: *As far as you know, was she seeing anyone in the ten month period that you shared a house with her?*

Response: *Well, yes, she did, but I wouldn't call any of them a relationship, as such... She was sort of seeing one until pretty recently. But like I said, I wouldn't call it a relationship.*

Question: *What can you tell me about it?*

Response: *Not a lot, really. I never met him and Mia didn't say much about it. I don't think she took it very seriously. Met him at a pub, I think, and... well, you know. It was just a thing.*

Question: *Yes, of course. Can you remember his name?*

Response: *God... No. She might have told me but if she did, I don't remember it.*

Question: *All right. If it does come back to you --*

Response: *Peter. That's it. I remember now. His name was Peter.*

Question: *How about a surname?*

Response: *No, she definitely never told me that.*

The interviewer went on to ask if Kat could recall any other information that might help identify the mysterious Peter, such as where he lived or his occupation, but to no end. Boyd recalled that other friends and fellow students at St. Martins had been asked about him, but none of them knew anything about the relationship.

Well, now the connection was made.

The phone interrupted her thoughts. "Okay, done," Nichols informed her. "Ten-thirty this morning work for you?" Boyd checked her watch. It gave her ninety minutes to get across the river.

She wasn't sure what pissed her off more, the smug look on Peter Greene's face or the fact that his solicitor was twenty minutes late. She was tempted to go ahead and start the interview, but anything she got now was certain to be excluded in the courtroom. So she sat there at the interview table, Detective Nichols at her side, pretending not to care.

"Looks like your counsel doesn't have a lot of time for you," Nichols said, if only to break the silence.

Peter just kept grinning.

"That's all right," the detective continued. "It gives me a chance to apologise for the accommodation."

"Yeah?"

"Yeah. But not to worry. We're working on getting you an upgrade to The Scrubs."

Boyd couldn't help smiling. The infamous Wormwood Scrubs was widely known as a violent hell hole, a hard time prison infested with rats, cockroaches, and the dregs of humanity. Its mention did manage to wipe the smirk off Peter's face, albeit temporarily.

"Sorry I'm late!"

The door opened and a birdlike man in a disheveled blue suit entered the room. In his mid-thirties, with a scruffy beard, he wore rimless glasses and was going prematurely bald. After a terse smile and a nod in the detectives' direction, he took a seat beside his client. "I hope you've respected Mister Greene's right to remain silent," he said.

"He's not exactly chatty," Nichols replied.

"Glad to hear it." He gave Peter a nod then reached across the table to offer Boyd a handshake. "Mark Bailey," he said with a smile. "I'll be representing Mister Greene."

Boyd introduced herself as the lead investigator and asked if he was ready to begin the interview.

"Absolutely." He placed his briefcase on the table. "Ready when you are."

Boyd activated the recording system and began by logging the time, date, location, and names of the four individuals in attendance. Then she paused, taking her time to fill her glass from the jug of water that was provided.

"Good morning, Mister Greene," she finally said, looking up at Peter. He looked to his solicitor for permission to speak, and got the nod.

"Yeah, hi," he said.

"Firstly," Boyd began. "I want you to be aware that this interview is being conducted in connection with the murder of Ms.

Mia Fraser, in Highbury, London, on the night of the twenty-third of September of last year. Is that clear for you?"

"Yeah, whatever."

"And I would also like you to be aware that you do not have to say anything. But it may harm your defence if you do not mention, when questioned, something which you later rely on in court. Anything you do say may be given in evidence. Do you understand that?"

Again, Peter looked to his solicitor and again got the go ahead. "Yeah, I got it," he said.

"Right then." Boyd forced a smile. "Let's start with the newspaper clippings that were found in a shoe box at the bottom of your wardrobe when you were arrested at 45 Strathan Close in East Putney yesterday morning."

"What about them?"

"Can you confirm that they are, in fact, your clippings?"

Peter looked to his solicitor for the third time, and once again he nodded. "Yeah, they're mine."

"You cut them out and kept them?"

"That's right."

"And you made certain notations on the clippings."

"Yeah, I wrote on them."

"Right," Boyd continued. "Can you explain why you would have done that."

"Not really," Peter replied.

"Would it be fair to say you had a special interest in the details of this crime?"

"I wouldn't say it is."

"All right. We can come back to that." She paused again. "Let's talk about the nature of your relationship with the victim."

"Who says I had one?"

"Did you know Mia Fraser?"

Another look to his solicitor and another nod. "Yeah, I knew her."

"Can you describe your relationship with her?"

The smirk took on a depraved bent. "How much detail do you want?"

Boyd met the look head on. "I take it from that response that you and Ms. Fraser had a sexual relationship. Is that correct?"

"Yeah, we had a sexual relationship," Peter replied. "She couldn't get enough of me."

"Until she dumped you," Nichols interjected.

"Who said she dumped me?"

"You were playing out of your league, mate. You got lucky one night and when she woke up she realised what a loser she'd hooked up with."

"You got no idea what you're talking about." Boyd noted that the smirk was gone, replaced by something resembling a scowl. "If anyone dumped anyone, it was me what dumped her."

"That's not what I've heard." Boyd picked up the interview again. "I heard she ended it."

"Well, that's bullshit. She probably told her friends that because she was embarrassed about it."

Both Boyd and Nichols were surprised by the duty solicitor's silence. They would usually make an objection here and there, even if groundless, if only to interrupt the flow of the interview. But this one seemed quite happy to sit back and listen.

"In fact," Boyd continued, "I have information that you were quite upset when Mia ended the relationship. So upset that you stalked her -- "

Bailey finally spoke up. "I don't think the word 'stalked' is quite appropriate," he said. "It has connotations that could be misleading."

"All right." Boyd turned back to Peter. "You were so upset that you waited outside the art college she attended and accosted her -- "

The solicitor piped up again. "Not sure about 'accosted' either."

"How about confronted?"

"Yes, I'm happier with that."

Boyd gave him a look and continued. "You confronted her as she left the college. Is that accurate?"

Peter shrugged. "Don't remember."

"Do you remember following her to a party and confronting her there? And by confronting, I mean you grabbed hold of her wrist and tried to forcibly remove her from the premises. Do you recall that episode?"

Peter, who was looking increasingly nervous, turned to his solicitor. "It's all right," he said. "Answer truthfully."

Peter shrugged. "We might'a had a little spat. You know. Like you do."

"Were you angry with her?"

"No," he lied. "I weren't angry. It was nothing. No big deal."

"Did you threaten to kill her?"

"What?! Hey, no! No way!" he turned to his lawyer. "They can't say that, can they? It's total bullshit!"

"I've spoken with an individual who claims that you threatened to kill Ms. Fraser. They said your exact words were..." Boyd read Ula's quote from the notes she made after their meeting. "...'If you're fucking somebody else, I'll fucking kill you both.' Did you say those words, Mister Greene?"

"No way! I never did!"

"Are you quite sure about that?"

Peter turned to his lawyer. "Are you gonna step in here, or what?"

"Yes." Bailey sat forward. "At this point, as it seems quite clear that you have decided to consider my client as a suspect, I'd like to assure you that Mister Greene had nothing to do with the gruesome murder of Ms. Fraser."

"Excuse us if we don't take your word for it," Nichols said.

The lawyer looked to Boyd. "Am I correct that he is being considered a suspect?"

"He's a person of interest," she replied.

"Well..." Bailey opened his briefcase. "Allow me to disabuse you of that interest." He removed two grainy black and white photographs and pushed them across the table.

"These images were taken by the security camera at the Ladbrokes betting shop on Putney High Street on the night of the murder. They clearly show that my client, Peter Greene, entered the shop at 8:47 PM and left the premises approximately three hours later, at 11:58 PM. Since Mia Fraser was murdered sometime between 10:15 and 10:40 PM, there is no conceivable way my client could be in any way involved in her death. So... Would you like to proceed with the interview, or shall we agree that it would be pointless to continue?"

27.

Dreams. Deep, dark, disturbing dreams, steeped in blood and charged with fear. Fragments of rain-soaked violence playing out in a random, disjointed narrative, the images too graphic, the sensation too powerful to be contrived. A dog barked, a scream pierced the night, and --

Ula sat up sharply, heart pounding, unable to catch her breath. It took a moment to process her surroundings. The four poster bed, the dancing clown print on the wall, the cane by the side of the bed. She took a deep breath, closed her eyes for a moment, then fell back onto the pillow and reached for her phone. Half past ten. How could that be? She never slept past eight o'clock, and even that was a rarity.

What day was it?

Monday, the phone said. Monday, the twenty-fifth of January. She tried to remember Sunday. What time had she gone to bed? It was a blank. In fact, most of the day was missing.

The piano. Ah, yes. She'd played *Moonlight Sonata*. How odd, she thought, to sit down, after all the years, and to play so effortlessly. But what then? What happened after that? The detective. That's right. She'd been rude, prying into things that had nothing to do with her. Private things from the distant past that are better left alone. Ula had many times considered destroying her mother's diary, along with all the other unpleasant reminders, but something had prevented her. Something she couldn't explain.

She suddenly realised that Erik was coming. In fact, he might already be in the house. He had a key to the front door, perhaps he'd let himself in and was already at work. Pulling herself out of bed, Ula threw some clothes on, picked up her cane, and went straight up to the loft.

It was dark and empty, the equipment undisturbed. Turning around, she made her way back down the stairway onto the first floor landing. Something made her stop in front of Mia's room. Pushing the door open, she half expected to see the young girl sitting at her drawing board, working on her latest project. She would look up and smile and say, "Hey, Ula. How's it going?" and Ula would smile back and say, "Fine. Would you like a cup of tea?"

Of course it was all a fantasy. Nothing remotely like that had ever happened. Not that Ula could remember, anyway. But it was a nice moment to think about anyway.

Erik wasn't in the kitchen, either, or out in the garden, having a smoke, as he sometimes did. It was strange, Ula thought. He'd never been late in the past. Why today, after he'd made such an effort to take control of the study? Why, on the day that he expected to start hosting Mia's memory, would he fail to appear?

A wave of panic took hold of her. What if he had decided that he no longer needed her? What if he planned to keep Mia's memory to himself, to continue the study without her? He was selfish and underhanded enough to do something like that. He'd certainly proved that he couldn't be trusted.

Her alarm grew as she dialled his number.

"Hello..." The familiar voice came on the line. *"This is the phone of Erik Berg. You may leave a message of any length after*

the tone. Please speak slowly and clearly and I will return the call at my earliest convenience. Thank you."

Ula hung up and stood there, frozen in thought. Be rational, she told herself. Don't jump to conclusions. Erik was an egotistical back-stabbing bastard, but he wouldn't be able to access Mia's memory files without the software. The security system she'd created would make it impossible to copy the programme and, on his own, Erik was incapable of re-creating it. Even if he went to someone who could -- if such a person existed -- it would take years of development to reach the level of sophistication she had achieved. No. Erik needed her as much as she needed him. Unless...

What if he'd stolen the programme disk at the same time he took Mia's memory drive? Given time, he would be able to figure out how to bypass its defences, and to build his own Impulse Receiver would be a relatively simple operation.

Moving as quickly as she could, Ula struggled up the stairs to the attic, her fears growing with each hobbled step. But as she approached the control panel her apprehension was replaced with bewilderment. Not only was the programme software intact, but Mia's memory drive was sitting on the worktop. A yellow post-it note was attached with two words written in big bold block letters:

YOU'RE WELCOME!

28.

"We arrive."

Nico pulled the car to the kerb in front of the house, turned the engine off, and killed the lights.

"Thanks," Mia said as she reached for the door. "Thanks for everything."

"No problem." The model flashed a smile. "You're okay now?"

"Yes, I'm fine, just really tired. But thanks again for your help." She started to open the door but Nico reached across and pulled it shut.

"You should stay," he said. "We can have a chat."

"Thanks, but I don't feel much like talking." His arm was pressing against Mia's breasts, his face so close she could smell the cheap cologne. "I'll see you at college," she said, feeling vaguely nauseous. "I just want to go in now."

"Tell me something." He sat back and withdrew his arm. "This asshole boy who makes the trouble. He was your boyfriend?"

"I guess so, more or less. But it's over now."

"Good." Nico looked her over. "Because you deserve something better than this."

Mia didn't want to be rude, but she was exhausted. "I'm sorry, Nico, but I'm not really up for talking right now. I appreciate everything you've done for me, but -- "

He moved closer. "Do you?"

"Do I what?"

"Appreciate what I have done."

"Yes, of course I do, but -- "

"Then you can show me."

Mia's heart started to beat wildly. "Show you what?"

"The appreciation."

"Hey... listen... I don't know what you thought was going to happen here, but -- "

Before she could complete the sentence, he reached over, grabbed her hand, and pulled it onto his hard cock, which he'd somehow managed to slip out of his trousers. Mia yanked her hand away.

"Jesus Christ! What's wrong with you?!"

"Hey, don't worry!" Nico smiled again. "You gonna like it, I promise." He tried to grab her hand again, but Mia shoved it away.

"Asshole!"

She fumbled for the door but he grabbed her by the collar, pulled her back toward him, and tried to kiss her. Mia clenched her fist and brought it around hard, landing a direct hit on the side of his face. It took a beat for the blow to register, then he exploded in anger.

"FUCKING BITCH!"

He reared back and delivered a hard backhand, his pinkie ring cutting a gash above her eye. As blood spilled out from the wound, Mia went for the door again, but he dragged her back in. Grabbing her by the scruff of the neck, he pushed her head down into his lap and thrust his pelvis up into her face.

"You wanna make it like this?" he snarled. "Okay! We make it like this!"

Mia tried to resist, but he was too strong. She flailed about, struggling to breathe, until she was spent, unable to fight back. Nico had her jeans down around her knees and was groping her panties when there was an almighty *CRASH!* and the driver's side window exploded inward, showering the interior of the car with a cascade of sparkling glass fragments.

"WHAT THE FUCK!"

Nico sprang bolt upright to find Ula standing at the window, wielding her cane like a bat, ready strike the next blow across the side of his head.

"Let her go," she said quietly.

"ARE YOU CRAZY?!!"

Ula stepped forward and swung again, this time shattering the windscreen.

"JESUS FUCKING CHRIST! WHAT'S WRONG WITH YOU?!!"

Ula brought the cane down yet again, this time blowing out the rear window.

"OKAY! OKAY!" Nico frantically reached across, opened the passenger side door, and pushed Mia out onto the pavement. *"GET THE FUCK OUT! GO!!"*

Scrambling for the ignition, he shoved the car into gear, and with a last indignant look at Ula, put his foot down and shot up the road, tyres squealing as the car spun around the corner and disappeared into the mist.

Ula lowered her cane and looked over at Mia, who was on the ground, sobbing as she pulled herself together. "You don't have to worry," she said in a whisper. "Nothing like this will ever happen to you again. I'm in control now."

29.

The day was not going well for Boyd. Following the disastrous Peter Greene interview, she headed back to Enfield, which meant sitting on the North Circular for roughly two hours, much of which was spent steaming over the duty solicitor -- whatever his name was -- for having set her up like that. The proper way to handle it would've been to take her aside before the interrogation began and show her the exculpatory evidence he'd uncovered. Of course, that would've robbed him of the story he'd be telling his colleagues over a pint that evening, recounting in full detail the look on the detectives' faces when he hit them with his client's air-tight alibi. The only consolation was knowing that the patently sick Peter Greene would be doing some significant hard time for the drug charges he still faced. Perhaps that would wipe the silly grin off his face once and for all.

The *PING* of an incoming text distracted her long enough that she failed to see the car in front come to stop. There was hardly a scratch on his rear bumper, but the driver -- a stocky northerner who claimed to be a driving instructor -- was concerned that there might be "untold internal damage to the vehicle" and insisted that he would have to "have me neck looked at by a doctor." Boyd didn't like using her badge in this sort of situation, but this guy was a tosser and she just wasn't in the mood, so she made sure he saw her credentials as she took out her licence. The man was suddenly very friendly and all his health and safety issues miraculously disappeared, as did he.

The text was from Nichols. Nothing consequential. Just *"thanks again for the coffee and let me know if I can do anything."* The two detectives had commiserated over a latte after leaving the detention centre, and though nothing was said openly, Nichols left little doubt that he would be keen to move their association into a more personal arena. As Boyd pulled her car back onto the road, she found herself entertaining various signals she could include in her response to the text, but quickly dismissed the exercise when she realised what she was doing. Timing is everything, she told herself again, and quite simply, this was not the right time.

Perhaps it was just a matter of bad timing for Mia Fraser, as well, she thought. A case of being in the wrong place at the wrong time. That scenario couldn't be ruled out, of course, but Boyd felt in her gut that the young girl's murder hadn't been some random act of violence. The killer was too careful in covering his tracks to be some arbitrary psycho with a knife. At any rate, with Peter Greene eliminated, it was back to square one.

Turning north off the Church Hill roundabout, Boyd decided to check in on Leonard before returning to the station. It was already half-past three and the school kids, in their blue and grey uniforms, were massing around the same sweet shop that she and her gang used to frequent, filling their bags with Jelly Babies, Kola Cubes, Black Jacks, and a dozen other sugary treats. She remembered it like it was yesterday.

The telly was on in the sitting room, but Leonard wasn't in his usual armchair. Or in the kitchen or the back garden. Boyd found him in his bedroom.

"What are you doing, Dad?"

"What does it look like I'm doing?"

"It looks like you're packing."

"That's right. I'm packing."

She could tell by the flat tone of his voice that he was in the midst of one of his episodes. "Are you going somewhere?" she asked.

He paused to look up, but his gaze went through her, as if he was talking to a ghost. "Don't you remember?"

"No, Dad." She sat down on the bed, beside the suitcase that he was filling with clothes. "I must've forgotten. Tell me."

"Your mum and I are going to Paris for the weekend. It's been in the works for ages. I did tell you, didn't I?"

"Are you sure it's this weekend, Dad?"

He smiled good-naturedly and continued to empty his wardrobe into the bag. "Of course I'm sure, sweetheart. Mum is very excited about it. You know, the Eiffel Tower and all that. To be honest, it's not really my thing. I'd just as soon go the football with the boys, but she deserves a bit of fun, don't you think?"

"Yes, of course I do."

Boyd knew from past experience not to challenge Leonard directly. It was best to lead him gently back into this world.

"Have you ever been to Paris?" she asked.

"No, darling. We always planned to go but we never got there. I wonder if I'll need a jacket and tie. I suppose I should bring one, just in case. You know what the French are like."

Boyd let a few moments pass before speaking again. "You know what mum once told me?" she said.

"What, darling?"

"She said that the best trip she ever took was the time you took her camping up in the Lake District."

"Did she really say that?"

"Yes. She said she thought she'd absolutely hate it but in the end it was wonderful. One of her favourite memories."

Leonard stopped packing and smiled as he looked back on the trip. "It was glorious weather. The sky so blue, sunlight on the water. Yes, I remember it very well."

"Mum said you two would go on long walks and not see anyone for the entire day. She even told me that you went skinny dipping."

Leonard smiled. "Yes, we did. And I'll tell you what. That water was absolutely perishing! I literally froze my nuts off!"

Boyd smiled. "It's good to know that she had all those lovely memories to carry her through the hard times."

Leonard paused. His smile dissipated and he looked over at Boyd, puzzled. "When did mum tell you all this?"

"When she was in hospital," Boyd replied. "A few days before she passed."

"A few days before..." Leonard sat down on the bed, looked over at his daughter, and attempted a smile. "Oh dear," he sighed.

Boyd leaned over to kiss his cheek. "I'll help you unpack," she said softly.

30.

The gentle warmth of the bath waters comforted Mia's bruised body, but did little to soothe her wounded spirit. How could she be such a bad judge of people? No, not people, she thought. Men. Since the age of fifteen, when she let that jerk Wyatt Hitch feel her up behind the Texaco station, she'd always picked the wrong guys. One after the other, they'd sweet-talked her into believing they were somebody they weren't, waiting to reveal their true character until they got what they were after. And this time the bastard didn't even bother with the sweet talk. Well, one thing was for sure. She would enjoy taking a razor to that painting she did of him. Or better yet, she'd scrawl *"POR-TRAIT OF A RAPIST"* in red paint across the top of the canvas and hang it in the school's entrance hall where everyone would see it. The idea made her smile.

Strange, she thought as she closed her eyes and let her head dip down below the water line. Before coming to England she hadn't been in a bath since she was a kid. Back home, baths were for children, a time to play with plastic sailboats and rubber duckies as you were scrubbed clean by the firm hand of a loving mother.

A sudden surge of homesickness engulfed Mia, bringing tears to her eyes. There was no way she could tell her parents about what had happened that night. Knowing them, they'd be on the next flight over, and they'd be carrying a one-way ticket home for her. Dad would be doing his "told you so" routine about life in the big city, while Mom would take a softer "we'd all feel a lot better if you could find a nice art college closer to home" kind of approach. Well, as much as she missed her family and life in Franklin, she wasn't about to go back with her tail between her legs. No way. She resolved to put the whole ugly episode behind her and focus like a laser on her art. After a year of struggling, she felt that she was on the verge of some kind of breakthrough and the last thing she needed was for this to throw her off track. She wouldn't even tell Kat what had happened.

Stepping out of the tub onto the cold tiles, she pulled a towel off the rack, quickly dried off, and slipped down the hall into her room. Grabbing "Teddy" from atop the chest of drawers, she wrapped him in her arms and curled up under the duvet, hoping to escape into a deep, dark sleep.

It started out as a dream. Mama's shadow standing over the bed, softly singing *Down in The Valley,* as she did every night when Mia was small and too scared of the dark to be alone.

> *"Roses love sunshine, violets love dew*
> *Angels in heaven know I love you.*
> *Know I love you, dear, know I love you*
> *Angels in heaven, know I love you..."*

"Hello, Mama," Mia said in the dream.

"Hello, baby. It's so nice to see you."

"It's nice to see you too, Mama. Why are you here?"

"I wanted to say that I'm sorry, baby. So sorry."

"Sorry about what, Mama?"

"That I wasn't there to protect you."

"You don't need to worry about me, Mama. I'm fine. Really."

"Good." Mama smiled down at her. "It makes me feel better knowing that. But we miss you something awful, baby. We'd give anything to have you back."

"I love you, Mama."

"I love you, too, baby. For always and forever..."

The gentle warmth of her mother's hand against her cheek filled Mia with a sense of inner peace. It was like being home again, in the safety of her own bed, where nothing bad could ever happen. But the feeling was short-lived. Something wasn't right. The touch went cold.

Opening her eyes, Mia gasped, then recoiled in horror and cried out. The shadowy figure that was standing over her took a quick step back, then turned and fled out the open door. Frozen with fear, Mia sat in the bed, gripping Teddy and shaking uncontrollably. The light in the hallway came on and Ula appeared at the door.

"Mia? What's happened?" She was doing up her dressing gown. "Are you all right?"

"I... I don't know..."

Ula stepped into the room. "What is it? Did you have a bad dream?"

"No... Someone was here. In the room. Watching me. They touched me... and when I woke up, someone was standing there."

"Are you sure you didn't imagine it?"

"Somebody was there. I'm sure of it."

"What exactly did you see?"

"Someone..."

"Who?"

"I don't know... It... it was too dark."

"Sometimes the mind can play tricks on you." Ula took another tentative step closer. "Would you like me to stay with you for a while?"

"No," Mia answered quickly. "No, I... I'm fine. It probably was dream." She shook her head and tried to smile. "I'll be fine. I just... I'm so tired. I just want to sleep."

"Yes, of course. You need to sleep." Ula backed out of the room, but stopped in the doorway. "If you need me, just call out."

"Yes, all right. I will. Thank you."

Ula withdrew and closed the door behind her. Mia waited a moment then slipped out of bed to quietly engage the lock. "It wasn't a dream, Teddy," she said as she took the bear in her arms and slid back under the covers. "I know it wasn't."

Flicking the bedside lamp on, she picked up her phone and checked the time. 3:12 AM. Four more hours of darkness.

31.

Searching the bed, Mia found her ringing phone under the pillow. "Hello?" she said without opening her eyes.

"What happened to you last night?" It was a relief to hear Kat's buoyant voice on the line. "You disappeared on me!"

"Oh..." Mia sat up and cleared her voice of sleep. "Sorry, I... I left early."

"Are you alone now?"

Mia reflexively looked around the room, just to be sure. "Yes," she replied "I'm alone. Why?"

"Someone said they saw you getting into some bloke's car. I thought maybe you -- "

"He just gave me a lift home."

"He?"

"Just some guy."

"Some guy?"

"Nobody."

"Hey, if you don't want tell me..."

Mia was silent for a moment. "His name is Nico," she finally said. "He's the one who invited us to the party. The model."

"Oh, right, the hot one. And...?"

Mia was silent, afraid that she'd start crying if she tried to speak. Kat picked up on it.

"Mia?" she said. "Are you all right?

"Yes... Yes, I'm fine."

"Are you crying?"

"Sort of."

"Why? Did something happen?"

"No, I..." Mia tried to lighten her tone, but it didn't work. "I'm just a bit moody, that's all."

"Mia..."

"It's fine, Kat. Really. I'm fine."

"I'm coming over."

"No!"

"You're obviously upset so I'm coming to see you."

"You really don't have to, Kat. I -- "

"I'm leaving right now."

"Okay," Mia sighed. "But not here."

"All right, where?"

Mia thought for a moment. "There's a pub on the corner. The Castle. I'll meet you there."

"I'm out the door," Kat said and hung up.

Mia knew it would take the better part of an hour for Kat to get there from Tooting, but she needed to get out of the house. Getting quickly dressed, she ran a brush through her hair and tiptoed down the stairway, hoping to slip out without being noticed.

"Do you realise that it's almost one o'clock?"

Mia spun around to find Ula standing in the kitchen doorway. "Ula! You startled me!"

"I was starting to think you'd sleep all day."

"Oh, right. Well, I, ah... I didn't sleep too well, so..."

"I'll make you a cup of tea," Ula said, heading back into the kitchen.

"Actually, Ula..." Mia followed her in. "I was thinking that I'd go out. Take a little walk. You know, get some air."

"Oh." The information seemed to throw Ula off balance. She stopped filling the kettle and set it down on the counter. "Right. Well, then... I'll go with you."

"Oh. That'd be nice, of course, but, well, if you don't mind, Ula, I'd kind of like to have some time on my own. You know, to clear my head a bit."

Ula frowned. "I was hoping we could talk," she said. "There are things I'd like to tell you... Things that you should know."

"Really? What things?"

"If we could just sit down for a few minutes, I can explain it all to you."

"Can we do it when I get back?"

Ula sighed in frustration. "Do you really feel the need to take this walk right now? I've been waiting to talk to you all morning!"

Mia hesitated, taken aback, and Ula seemed to realise that she'd gone too far.

"I'm sorry," she quickly backtracked. "I'm being unreasonable. I didn't mean to be. In fact, just the opposite. It's just that..." She paused and shook her head, as if answering a question that she herself had raised. "No. You should have your walk. Yes. You go for a walk and clear your head. We can talk afterwards." She smiled. "Go ahead. It's fine."

"If you're sure you don't mind."

"I just said that I didn't."

"Yes, all right. Good. I'll, ah... I'll see you later then. We can talk when I get back."

Ula followed her to the entrance hall and waited as she put her coat on. "Don't be long," she said as Mia went through the door.

It was half past two by the time Kat walked into The Castle. She found Mia at a corner table, nursing a pot of Jasmine tea.

"Sorry, babe! Traffic was a bitch! I should've taken the -- " She stopped short when she saw the bruises on Mia's face. "Oh my god! What happened to you?"

Mia shrugged. "Turns out the model wasn't exactly a gentleman."

"No! Did he...?"

"He tried to."

"Bastard!" Kat sat opposite and Mia filled her cup with tea. "Christ, Mia! What happened?"

"He gave me a lift home but when we got there he wouldn't let me out of the car. Then he just turned on me."

"Fuck! I hope you kicked him in the balls so hard they turned to soup!"

Mia smiled. "I don't know about that but I did find blood under my finger nails this morning."

"What did you do? I mean, did you just fight him off?"

Mia started to answer, but hesitated, suddenly unsure if she could trust her memory of the event. Had Ula really saved her or was that part of some troubled dream she'd had that morning as she slept?

"I don't know," she said. "It's all a bit of a blur."

Kat reached across the table to take Mia's hand. "The important thing is, you got away, and you're all right."

Mia nodded, then shook her head. "It was stupid of me. I'm too trusting."

"Don't do that, Mia! It's absolutely not your fault! Any man who did what he did is a king-sized asshole and you are not allowed to blame yourself!"

"You're right. I know you're right."

"Of course I am. Are you gonna be okay?"

"Yeah. I think so. I mean, sure. Of course."

"You're not convincing me, babe."

Mia scrunched up her face. She really did not want to start crying again. "It's just... It was a pretty strange night. In more ways than one."

"Why, what else?"

"I'm not really sure, but..."

"But what? Not sure about what?"

Mia leaned in and lowered her voice. "I think Ula came into my room last night. While I was sleeping."

"What?"

"I think she was watching me sleep. And then she touched me."

"Touched you? Jesus Christ!" Mia gave her a look and she lowered her voice. "Touched you where?"

"No, not like that. Just here, on the cheek." Mia demonstrated. "It woke me up."

"I told you, didn't I? She's a fucking weirdo!"

"I know, I know."

"What did she say when you woke up?"

"Nothing. I screamed and she ran off. Then she came back and tried to convince me it was all a dream."

"Mia..." Kat leaned forward and waited for Mia to meet her eyes.

"What?"

"You have to get out of there!"

"I know I probably should, but... I was so lucky to find that place."

"Listen to me, sweetie. I don't care how convenient or cheap that place is. You have to leave. I mean, come on, there really is something seriously wrong with that woman."

"I don't know. Maybe I'm making too much of it."

"Stop it, Mia! Because there is no way on earth I'm going to allow you to stay in that house with that woman. What you're going to do is come stay with me until we can sort something out."

"That's really so nice of you, Kat, but -- "

"Stop! It's settled. You're moving to Tooting. I have an air mattress you can sleep on."

"What about your housemates?"

Kat made a face and paused to think. It was true that she couldn't just show up with a new housemate. "I'll talk to them tonight," she said. "And we'll move you in tomorrow."

"What should I say to Ula?"

"Did you give her a deposit?"

"No."

"Then you don't even have to tell her anything. We'll just grab your stuff and get you the hell out of there!"

Mia nodded. "Maybe it's for the best."

"Of course it is! All you have to do is make it through one more night."

32.

The sun had set and thunder was rolling in the distance as Mia stepped onto the portico and approached the front door. It took a moment to steady herself and slip the key into the lock, an effect of Kat's insistence that they ditch the jasmine tea in favour of a series of Happy Hour cocktails. They'd had a good laugh -- which was the point -- but Mia's restored spirit dissipated on the walk across the park, replaced by a growing sense of dread that coalesced in the pit of her stomach as she eased the door open and stepped into the entrance hall.

Aside from a soft light emanating from the back of the house, the place was in total darkness. Resisting the temptation to slink up the stairs to the safety of her room, Mia hung her jacket on the hall rack, took a deep breath, and headed for the kitchen.

Ula was sitting at the table, bowed head in her hands. "That was a long walk," she said without looking up.

"Yeah, I just kept going." Hoping to make a quick escape, Mia hovered in the doorway. "Made it all the way to Hampstead Heath and back. I feel a lot better now."

"I'm happy for you," Ula replied coldly, still hiding her face.

"Listen, Ula, I -- "

"I really hope you're not going to apologise again!" Ula lifted her head to fix Mia with a searing look. "Because that's really getting quite worn out!"

Her anger was palpable, but there was something in her expression -- an underlying vulnerability -- that made Mia feel a bit sorry for her. She took a tentative step into the room.

"I... I don't know what to say, Ula. I wasn't thinking and I lost track of time. I really *am* sorry!"

"Have I done something to offend you?"

"No..."

"Or to make you hate me?"

"Of course not!"

"Then why are you lying to me?"

"What do you mean? Lying about what?"

"You went for a long walk? To Hampstead?"

"Yes."

"That's what you were doing all this time?"

"Yes, I told you -- "

Ula slammed both fists down on the table and cried out: *"LIAR!"*

The sudden outburst shocked both women and charged the room with a long, precarious silence. Ula finally let out a deep sigh, reached for her cane, and pulled herself up from the table.

"I'm sorry..." she said, taking a tentative step in Mia's direction. "I told myself not to do that, but I just... I lost control. It was wrong of me, but it's only because I'm worried about you. About your safety."

"Ula... I mean, it's nice, but... We're just housemates, right? Nothing more. You don't have to look after me."

"Yes, well. There are things that you don't understand. Things that I need to explain to you."

"What things?"

Ula gave her a reproachful look. "You didn't go for a walk, did you?"

"Yes, like I said -- "

"No, Mia!" She paused. "You didn't. You met that friend of yours at the pub and you've been sitting there, drinking and laughing the entire time you've been gone. That's what you did."

"Ula..."

"Please don't try to deny it because I'm afraid that will just make me angry again and..." She took a deep breath in an attempt to tamp down her rising emotions. "It's very important that we discuss these issues in a calm, reasonable manner, no matter how upsetting they may be."

"I really don't know what you're talking about," Mia said, feeling increasingly agitated. "But you need to tell me how you know that I met up with Kat."

Ula produced a nervous smile. "At least you admit it now. That's an improvement."

"Have you been following me?"

"No." She shook her head. "At least, not like you mean it."

"Then how? How did you know what I was doing?"

"Because..." Ula tried to speak in a soft, soothing voice, but the words were coming out strained, full of all her suppressed anxiety. "You see... It might sound strange, but... well, we're together now. Wherever you go and whatever you do, you carry me with you. And from this moment on, I will always be with you. Looking out for you."

Mia stared at Ula in disbelief. Kat had been right all along. She was insane. Completely and utterly stark raving mad.

"No," Ula said. "I'm not mad."

"I didn't say -- "

"You didn't have to. You see..." Her smile disappeared and she became deadly serious. "I know everything about you. Even what you're thinking."

"This is crazy..." Mia whispered.

"I know, it must be confusing for you. But I can explain. If we could just sit down together... I'll make us a nice cup of tea and we can have a chat..." She moved to the counter, grabbed the kettle and started to fill it with tap water. "What would you like? I'm having normal, but I can make jasmine for you."

"Listen, Ula, thanks but I..." Mia eased toward the door. "I think I'll just go on up to bed. Maybe we can talk in the morning."

"No, wait!"

But Mia was already out the door. Ula followed into the hallway, calling out from the bottom of the stairs as Mia climbed the steps. "Please, Mia, come back! You mustn't be alone tonight!"

"I really have no idea what you're talking about, Ula, but you're making me extremely uncomfortable!"

"I'm sorry!" Ula limped up the stairway, taking the steps one-by-one as quickly as she could. "I don't mean to upset you but it's very important that I explain the situation to you!"

Mia tried to close the door, but Ula caught up at the last moment and blocked it with her cane. "Let me in," she said as they eyed each other through the gap. "I can explain everything."

"Were you in my room last night?"

"What...?"

"Were you watching me while I slept?"

"That's irrelevant... I'm trying to explain to you -- "

"Why would you do that?"

"I... I'm trying to help you, Mia."

"I don't want your help. Please go away."

Ula sighed in frustration. "If you would just give me a chance..."

Without warning, she surged forward, using all her pent up energy to shove Mia out of the way. Quickly slipping into the room, she turned the key in the door, removed it, and gripped it tightly in her fist.

"What are you doing!" Mia cried out.

"Please stay calm and listen carefully to what I'm going to tell you."

"Open the door!"

"If you'll just listen to me, I will."

"Open it now!"

"Please try to focus, Mia. It's important that you understand the situation."

"Why are you doing this?!"

"I'm trying to keep you safe."

"Safe?"

"Yes."

"Safe from *what!*"

Ula closed her eyes and took a deep breath. "Something is supposed to happen tonight. Something horrible. But if we stay here, together, locked in this room, we can prevent it. We can change the course of events."

"You're not making any sense!" Mia was close to tears now. "None of this makes sense!"

A sudden sad melancholy came over Ula. She tilted her head to the side and took a step forward. "Mia... Poor Mia. You have no idea, do you?"

"You're scaring me, Ula. Please stop it."

"It's so difficult... So hard to say it..."

"Just go away... *please!*"

But Ula wasn't listening. She was deep in thought, trying to formulate a way to tell Mia that she was already dead. That she had been brutally murdered four months earlier and if she was allowed to go out onto the street, someone would be waiting for her and it would happen all over again.

"Do you know those strange feelings that you've been having?" she finally said. "That sense that somebody is watching you? It's always the same, isn't it? When you look around, no one is there."

"Is it some kind of mind trick, like when you knew what number I was thinking of?"

"No, it's not a trick. Not really."

"Then how?"

"Do you remember the dream you had last night? What is that song your mother sings to you? The one about the roses and the angels."

"How are you doing this?!!"

"You see, it's me that you've been sensing. I'm the one who's been watching you, but not from the outside. I'm inside you, Mia. Inside your thoughts... Your memory, to be precise. That's where I am right now. In your memory. That's where we both are."

Mia took a step back and puts her hands up, as if to ward off what was to come. Ula took an equal step forward.

"I think that deep down, you know the truth."

"No..."

"But it doesn't have to happen the way it did before!" Ula was feverish now, overflowing with passion. "Don't you see? You're living through me! I'm hosting your memory and I've learned how to change the way things happen!"

"No, Ula, please stop!"

"It's all right!" she said. "This time can be different! This time you don't have to die!"

A sudden *FLASH OF LIGHT* and a *CLAP OF THUNDER* distracted Ula long enough for Mia to grab the lamp off the bedside table. She yanked it out of the wall and swung it around in one movement, striking Ula's temple with the metal base. As she fell to the floor, unconscious, the room key fell out of her hand.

Mia didn't hesitate, or stop to see what damage she'd done. She unlocked the door, flew down the stairs and out the door. Onto the street.

33.

"Shit!"

As she reached for her phone Mia realised that it was in her jacket, which was hanging on the hall rack. Her wallet and her keys were in the same pocket.

Standing in front of the house -- breathless, trying not to panic -- the rain came. A few drops at first, then a sudden downpour, bombarding the pavement with a barrage of tiny explosions and drenching Mia in a virtual torrent of water. Get to The Castle, she thought. Someone there will lend her a phone so she can call Kat.

The park was dark and ominous, but it was the quickest route. Following the tree-lined walkway, lit by a few dim street lamps, Mia walked briskly at first, mind racing, then broke into a nervous run, splashing through muddy puddles that were forming in every dip along the path.

Ula had scared the shit out of her. She'd clearly gone off the deep end, but it was even weirder than that. Okay, she could've easily followed her to the pub and seen her drinking with Kat, but how about the other stuff? Ula seemed to know everything that she'd been thinking and feeling. She'd even invaded her dreams! Maybe it was just clever guesswork or some kind of crazy mind manipulation, like magicians do. But then again...

There was something deep down, in the far reaches of Mia's psyche, that frightened her to the core of her being. What if it wasn't a trick, she thought. What if, in some inexplicable way, Ula was telling the truth and this was all some nightmarish dream that she couldn't wake up from? Things hadn't felt right for some time. Not since arriving at the house on Highbury Crescent, two weeks earlier. And there were the blank spots -- moments, hours, and even days that simply didn't exist, at least not that she could recall, no matter how hard she tried. Even now, running through the darkened park in the rain, there was that persistent feeling of deja vu. Ula's words echoed in her mind.

"This time you don't have to die."

The storm ended as abruptly as it began, leaving behind a heavy mist that hung in the air like a silky veil, softening the line between earth and sky and melting the distant city lights into halos of formless colour. Veering off to take a shortcut through the playground, Mia slipped on a patch of wet leaves and hit the ground hard, knocking the air out of her lungs. As she lay there on her back, struggling to draw a breath, something caught her eye. A sudden movement. A sound.

Rolling onto her stomach and pushing herself off the ground, she knelt on the wet grass and surveyed the surrounding darkness. A small animal perhaps? Or a tree branch swaying in the wind? Why had she come through the park? How could she have been so stupid!

Suddenly, she was walking. Wide awake, alert, constantly checking over her shoulder, aware of every movement and every vibration in the air. A dog barked, a distant siren wailed, and she noticed the sound of heavy breathing. It was near. Was it her own?

Another movement, a fleeting glimpse of a figure in a hooded jacket, and he was suddenly upon her. The echo of a scream, the flash of a long blade, and then the blood. So much blood.

The end came quickly for Mia. There was no pain this time, and no tears, as there had been the first time. She lay on the ground, perfectly still and quiet, peacefully thinking her final thoughts as the world got darker and darker, and finally disappeared, leaving only the void. The last byte in Mia's memory file contained the comforting sound of her mother's voice.

"Roses love sunshine, violets love dew
Angels in heaven know I love you.
Know I love you, dear, know I love you
Angels in heaven, know I love you..."

34.

Experiencing Mia's murder delivered a crushing blow to Ula's spirit. Upon emerging from the memory she frantically paced the house, wandering from room to room, unable to organise her movements, let alone her thoughts. The images that filled her head were vague and elusive, as the memories always were, but they were vivid enough to upset the delicate balance that had long existed in her psyche, a symmetry that, up until now, had allowed her to function as a rational human being.

Most elusive was the face. Like a distant star that disappears when you attempt to look directly into its light, the killer's features vanished into darkness when Ula tried to summon the image. Perhaps Mia never knew the identity of her attacker. Or perhaps her mind's final act was to block the traumatic details from being copied to her memory. In the end, it didn't matter. Whatever the reason, the killer was no less anonymous now than he had been before all her efforts. But that wasn't the source of Ula's distress. Her anguish came from the knowledge that she had failed to protect Mia from having to experience her death a second time. In fact, it was worse than that. Not only had she been unable to change the outcome, her own actions had effectively pushed Mia into the arms of her assassin.

With these disturbing thoughts bouncing around in her head, Ula felt the need to escape the confines of four walls and soon found herself walking in the park, heading toward the site where Mia had taken her last breath.

The western sky was flush with pink and gold, the air brisk with a winter freeze as she approached the spot, which showed no sign of what had occurred four months earlier. The flowers, sympathy cards, and silver balloons that had covered the area in the days following the event had quickly dwindled down to a few bouquets from distant friends and family, then finally disappeared altogether, leaving nothing but the long shadows, cast by now barren trees.

Something about being there, standing over the earth that had absorbed Mia's life blood, inspired a sense of calm in Ula. There was a connection between them, a link so strong that even death couldn't weaken it. She stared into the hard ground and thought about the first time she'd stood there, on that terrible September morning. It was just before dawn, as the day's first light was breaking, that the doorbell rang.

"I'm sorry to disturb you," the woman had said, flashing a police badge. "I'm Detective Inspector Sarah Boyd. May I ask who I'm speaking with?"

"My name?"

"Yes, your name."

"Ula... Ula Mishkin."

"I apologise again for disturbing you, Ms. Mishkin, but we've had a major incident in the area and we're making enquiries throughout the neighbourhood. I wonder if I could ask you a few questions."

"What kind of incident?" Ula asked sleepily.

"We're attempting to identify the victim of a serious crime. I see that this property is a single family dwelling. May I ask how many individuals occupy the premises?"

Ula noticed the flashing blue lights of several police cars on the opposite side of the park. "Just me," she said. "And my housemate. But she's not here right now."

"Do you know her current whereabouts?"

"No, I... I was asleep and... Her room is empty but I don't know where she is."

"I see. Well, there's probably no reason for concern, but can you describe your housemate for me?"

"Yes, she's... she's American," Ula said haltingly. "From the south. Her name is Mia. Mia Fraser. Has something happened to her?"

"Do you know Ms. Fraser's age?" Boyd asked.

"Nineteen, I think. She's a student. She rents a room from me."

"I understand. And are you aware of any distinguishing characteristics on your housemate?"

"Distinguishing characteristics?"

"Such as a scar or a tattoo?"

"She has a tattoo. On her ankle. A small red rose." Ula could see the detective's demeanour change as soon as she said it.

"I see." She paused. "Ms. Mishkin, I'm sorry to inform you that there's a very good chance that your housemate has been the victim of a very serious attack. I'm going to ask you to get dressed and accompany me to the scene of the crime."

"The scene of the crime?"

"Yes. I'd like you to verify the victim's identity."

The detective didn't offer any more information and Ula didn't ask questions as they crossed the park to the site, which had been cordoned off with police crime tape. When she was ready, Detective Boyd nodded and a man in a white jumpsuit and purple gloves stepped forward to pull the heavy plastic sheet back, only far enough to reveal Mia's face. She looked at peace, Ula thought, as if in the midst of some pleasant dream.

"Ms. Mishkin," Boyd said after a moment.

"Yes?"

"Are you able to identify the victim as your housemate, Mia Fraser?"

Ula remembered her legs going weak and her mouth feeling numb as she whispered, "Yes... Yes, that's Mia."

Walking back across the park in the last light of the day, Ula felt more clear-headed, able to think again. Her failure to alter the past had been traumatic and depressing and painful, but it wasn't absolute. If she'd learned anything from her explorations into Mia's mind, it was that memory provided a flexible interpretation of the past. But it was now equally clear that manipulating those memories into a desired outcome would not be a simple task. In the way the subconscious makes its own rules and creates its own narrative in a dream, it was Ula's subconscious that was diverting Mia's memory. She was able to change events, but not necessarily in the way her conscious mind intended. At least, not yet.

Unlocking the front door, she entered the hallway and climbed the staircase to the first floor landing. Perhaps she'd failed this time, she thought, but there was no limit to the number of visits she could make to the memory. Now that the cache that contained that night had been located, she could target it as many times as required, reshaping events over and over until she reached a satisfactory outcome.

But she was spent. With a few hours sleep she could return to the E.I.R. and start over, fresh. Feeling a renewed sense of optimism, Ula quickly undressed, slipped into bed, and lay on her back waiting for sleep to come. However long it took, she would never allow Mia's memory to die.

35.

Boyd leaned back in her chair and re-read Nichols' text for the umpteenth time. *"thanks again for the coffee and let me know if I can do anything."* It didn't really require a response, but it seemed rude to ignore it. A simple *"thanks, I'll do that"* would suffice, but a perfunctory reply like that would surely put an end to the communication, and Boyd wasn't quite sure she was ready to do that. She needed something that wouldn't shut him down entirely, but wouldn't seem overly eager, either.

Shaking her head at her own indecisiveness, Boyd set the phone aside and went back to the Fraser file, which she was reviewing from front to back, hoping to pick up something she'd previously missed. It was, no doubt, a pointless exercise -- she'd been through it all at least a half dozen times before -- but the Peter Greene fiasco had renewed her determination to find some angle that she could pursue.

"Cuppa?"

Leonard appeared at the door in his pyjamas and dressing gown, two mugs of tea in hand.

"I thought you were in bed hours ago," Boyd said, checking her watch to see that it was half past midnight.

"Couldn't sleep..." Leonard handed her one of the mugs and eased into the old armchair Boyd had placed beside the desk to accommodate her father's visits. "And it looks like the same goes for you."

"Just going over an old case," Boyd replied, gesturing toward the file. "What's your excuse?"

"Age, love. Old age." He smiled and took a sip of tea. "Old bladder, to be specific."

"Well, cheers." Boyd saluted her father with the tea. "Nice to have the company."

Leonard nodded, then sat back and shook his head. "Funny about that Paris business," he mused. "I reckon if you hadn't got home when you did, I'd be wandering around the Champs Elysées right now, wondering where your mum had got to."

"I don't know. I think you would've -- "

"Come to my senses?"

Boyd shrugged. "You could've picked a worse place to disappear to than Paris."

"Yes, well, who knows what it'll be next time." He gave her a look, but she frowned and he got the message. "So what're you working on?" he asked, moving on to another subject.

"Oh, it's the Mia Fraser murder case," she replied. "Do you remember -- "

"The young American girl in Highbury Fields. Yes, tragic, that one."

She nodded. "Also exasperating."

"No leads?"

"I thought I had him, but it seems he's got an air tight alibi."

"Oh, that's annoying. What's your theory of the case?"

"I'm afraid I haven't got one."

"Well, there's your problem. You need a theory."

Boyd shrugged. "There's not enough evidence to build a theory."

"Then use your gut."

"My gut?"

"That's right. What does your gut say?"

Boyd frowned. "I don't know. I think -- "

"Don't think, darling! Feel! What do you feel?"

"I don't know, Dad, I..." She hesitated. Leonard's outdated methods wasn't how modern police work was approached, but she couldn't very well say that, so she settled on, "I just don't work that way."

"No, you don't, do you? Never did, either. Always needed to think it through six ways from Sunday. Like your mum." Leonard sighed. "Me? I'm a gut instinct kind of guy, and you know what? It's a pretty good prognosticator. Not a hundred percent, of course, but it's right a fair bit of the time. You know, weighing things up, taking your time to put all the pieces of the puzzle in place, that's all very well. But you can overthink things, too."

"I suppose you're right," Boyd said, not very convincingly.

Leonard took a last gulp of tea and vacated the chair. "And I'm not just talking about police matters, either," he said.

Boyd gave her father a long look. "And what makes you think there are other matters I'm overthinking?"

"My gut," he said, with a wink.

"Oh, yeah? Well, I guess maybe you do have a pretty good gut."

"Good gut, weak bladder." He smiled, gave her a kiss on the forehead, and said good night, adding a fatherly, "Don't stay up too late!" as he went through the door.

Boyd shook her head, reached for the phone, and read Nichols' text yet again. "*thanks again for the coffee and let me know if I can do anything.*"

"Fuck it!" she said out loud and quickly tapped out a reply. *"You're very welcome. Let's do it again sometime."*

Holding her breath, she hesitated for only the briefest of moments before hitting send. "All right, Detective," she said out loud. "The ball's in your court."

Feeling simultaneously foolish and exhilarated, it took Boyd less than a minute to start second-guessing the move. What if she'd misinterpreted the signals and he was just being polite? He might look at the message and wonder why on earth she would suggest they have another coffee? How unprofessional that would be. And how embarrassing!

"Ahhh!"

Setting the phone aside, Boyd starting going through the file again. The autopsy, the statements, the gruesome photographs, she'd seen it all before and the only thing it added up to was a big question mark. Closing the folder, she leaned back and shut her eyes. Perhaps Leonard was right, she thought. Perhaps she was allowing reason to get in the way of a case that had no basis in logic.

Ula Mishkin came to mind.

Mia's friend, Katherine Ellis, had insisted that Ula must've had something to do with the murder, but her only rationale was that she was 'an extremely weird person.' Mishkin was an odd one, all right, there was no denying that, but it's a big leap from socially awkward to brutal killer. It couldn't be discounted, of course, but even if you set aside her physical disability, she had no discernible motive to commit such a cold-blooded act, and there was absolutely no evidence to link her to the crime. Still.

In some obscure way, Boyd felt that Ula was the key to the puzzle.

Remembering the diary she'd found on Ula's bookcase, Boyd opened her laptop and entered the search term, "Olga Mishkin." Nothing of interest came back, just a few Facebook and LinkedIn pages belonging to unrelated people. After several more unsuccessful searches using various filters, with her curiosity aroused, Boyd logged into the Met Police archives and found a 1996 file marked "Mishkin, Olga." Inside the folder was a single photocopied page of an officer statement, a report from the coroner, and several newspaper articles. Boyd clicked on one from *The Times:*

MOTHER AND CHILD IN MURDER-SUICIDE

London, 12 October. Russian immigrant Olga Mishkin woke early on Thursday morning, removed her six year-old son, Aleksi, from his bed, placed him in a warm bath, and held his head under water until he drown. She then stood on a step ladder, placed a noose around her neck, and stepped to her own death.

The pair were discovered in their North London home by the deceased boy's twin sister, Ula, who had been asleep in the bed next to her brother. No note was left by the widowed mother and police are at a loss to explain her actions, except to

say that she had suffered from mental illness for
several years.

Boyd sat back and contemplated the significance of the information. Her phone pinged with an incoming text, but she was
too absorbed to notice.

36.

Flicking the bedside lamp on, Ula sat up and reached for the phone. 3:47 AM. Uncertain how long she'd been asleep, she recalled returning home from the park at sunset, which would've been around six o'clock. She'd gone straight to bed, meaning she must have slept for close to ten hours. Why then did she feel so exhausted?

Pulling on a baggy jumper and tracksuit bottoms, she made her way downstairs and was surprised to find the kitchen lights burning brightly. Strange, she thought. She never used the overhead lights, preferring the subdued glow of the oven lamp instead. It was disconcerting, but after checking that the front and back doors were secure, she dismissed her apprehensions and filled the kettle.

As she sat alone at the kitchen table, eating dry toast and sipping black tea, Ula looked around the room and lamented her reality. Leaving it behind wouldn't be difficult. There was simply nothing here for her. Nothing left to lose.

The plan had taken shape as she lay in bed the previous evening, waiting for sleep to come. There were practical concerns, of course, but nothing that couldn't be arranged. A regular supply of pentobarbital would be needed to keep her in a drug-induced coma, and a daily caretaker would be required -- someone she could trust to administer and monitor the dose. Nourishment and bodily functions would have to be seen to, as well, but it would be easy enough to set up a basic life support system of feeding tubes and catheters. All this would come at a substantial cost, of course, but Ula had a plan for that, too.

The property on Highbury Crescent had cost her mother one hundred and eighty-seven thousand pounds when it was purchased in 1989. It had come as a shock when Erik told her it would now be worth somewhere in the neighbourhood of three million. Although broke and in need of some sort of income, at the time she couldn't imagine having to leave the house she'd lived in for her entire life, which was why Erik arranged for her to rent the room to Mia. But things were different now. Everything had changed. Now, it would be a relief to get out of her present circumstances.

Ula smiled as she imagined a picturesque one bedroom cottage, somewhere out of the way -- perhaps by the sea, or in some deep, dark forrest. It would be no more than a repository for her physical body, of course, but she liked the idea of the sound of waves crashing against the rocks, or a symphony of morning birdsong filtering through to her new life. Perhaps her subconscious could even impose the cottage onto Mia's memory and they could live there together, taking long walks on the beach before returning to their little kitchen to make pasta and drink red wine.

Ula's excitement grew as she hobbled up the narrow attic staircase, heart beating faster in anticipation of spending the next few hours with Mia. While her conscious mind wasn't yet able to control the way the past would unfold, she was confident that by replaying the events of that night over and over, she would learn to guide the narrative to a more acceptable outcome. Once Mia survived the night, there would be no limit to the new memories they could create together.

Unlike most of us, who hold hopes and dreams for the future in our heart, Ula had long ago lost the ability to conceive of better days ahead. But while the rest of us have no choice but to live with the unalterable regrets we've accumulated through the years, Ula had found a way to apply her hopes and dreams to the past. She and Mia would become one, producing new memories from old, creating a new life together, safe from the destructive influences of the physical world. The idea lifted her spirit to a height she had never before experienced, giving her, for the first time ever, a feeling of unrestrained exhilaration about what was to come.

Flicking the attic lights on, Ula froze in horror as she took in what lay before her. The Electronic Impulse Receiver, the mainframe computer, the monitoring station... it was all strewn across the floor in a twisted mesh of smashed plastic, crushed glass, pieces of metal, and stray bits of coloured wire. Even the subject chair had been overturned and battered with the sledgehammer that lay in the midst of the wreckage.

Ula just stood there, numbly taking in the utter destruction of all that she had worked so long and hard to create. It might have been just a few moments, but perhaps it was longer before the true horror of what had happened sunk in. Forgetting her cane, she rushed forward and fell to her knees, searching frantically through the rubble. A long anguished cry escaped from the depths of her soul when she found it. The hard drive that contained all that was left of Mia had been crushed by one cruel, devastating blow. She was truly gone now. The memory of her

thoughts and feelings, the impulses that made her what she was -
- and what she could have been -- were lost forever. It was as if
the final act in her brutal, heartless murder had taken place.

Lost in her grief, Ula didn't at first notice the scrap of paper
that lay amongst the wreckage. When she finally looked up and
saw the message that had been left for her, it sent a chill up her
spine.

Written in big, bold letters were the words:

STUPID GIRL!

37.

Boyd woke at 4 AM, for no apparent reason other than a sense that something was terribly wrong. Getting out of bed and slipping into her dressing gown, she went straight to Leonard's room to find the light on and the bed empty.

"Dad?"

She called out as she quickly checked the kitchen and sitting room, only to find them both empty. Relieved that the front door was still locked and the chain securely fastened, she became aware of a current of cold air drifting through the house. Hitting the overhead light switch, she discovered that the sliding door onto the patio had been left wide open.

"Dad?"

There was no response, but she could hear the sound of soft sobbing coming from the bottom of the garden. As she approached, she saw that Leonard was sitting hunched over, head bowed, in one of the two faded Adirondack chairs that had been there for as long as she could remember.

"Dad?" she softly repeated as she approached. "Are you all right?"

"Yes, darling..." He looked up and wiped his eyes with the palm of his hand. "I'm fine. Go back inside."

Boyd pulled her dressing gown tight against the cold and sat on the edge of the empty chair. "Do you want to talk about it?"

Leonard shook his head and took a deep breath. "Embarrassing, in't it? Seeing your old man in this state?"

"No, Dad. Of course it's not. I understand."

"I'm not feeling sorry for myself," he said. "It's not that."

"I know..."

He shook his head and sighed. "I just... I woke up and there I was, crying like a baby. No idea why." He attempted a smile. "Not a clue."

"A dream perhaps?"

"Yes. Perhaps I had a dream. You must be cold, sweetheart."

"No, dad, I'm fine."

"Are you sure? It's bloody freezing out here."

Boyd shook her head and looked up into the clear winter sky. It was teeming with stars -- some still burning brightly, others no more than an echo of a long extinguished light traveling to earth through a cold, dark universe.

"Beautiful, isn't it?" Leonard said.

"Yes." Boyd smiled. "Beautiful."

They sat there, staring into the heavens, for several minutes before Leonard sighed and shifted in his seat. "I've been thinking about Trevor," he said quietly.

"It was good that you got to spend some time together. I'm sure it meant a lot to him."

Leonard nodded. "Want to know what we talked about?"

"If you want to tell me."

"Football," he said with a smile.

"Football?"

Leonard shrugged. "He wanted to know the scores. Imagine that. Being on your death bed and the one thing on your mind is how Tottenham did against Chelsea."

"That's dedication."

"Oh, Trevor was a fan, all right. Ever since we were lads. He was Tottenham and I was Arsenal."

"Nothing wrong with a little friendly rivalry."

"Not always friendly."

"What happened between the two of you?" Boyd asked.

"You know, darling, the truth is I really don't know. Thinking back on it, it seems as though one day it was all fine and the next day we weren't speaking. It couldn't have been like that, of course, but I'll be damned if I know what started it off. I just can't for the life of me remember what it was."

"Does it matter?"

"I suppose not. What's done is done, and it can't be undone, so best to leave it alone. That's the answer, isn't it?"

"I think it is, Dad."

"Anyway, we haven't much choice, do we?"

"No, we don't."

Leonard smiled, then reached across and patted his daughters knee. "Now let's get inside and have a nice, warm cuppa."

As they crossed the garden toward the house, Boyd could hear her phone ringing.

38.

Aleksi knew his sister better than she knew herself. Every thought, feeling, pathetic fear, and pitiful emotion that ever passed through her fragile mind had come straight to him -- and he ensured that it remained a one way street. As brilliant as Ula was, he saw her for the frightened little girl she'd always been, easy to deceive and effortlessly manipulated. At least, until recently. Her ridiculous infatuation with the art student not only made her look foolish, it threatened the lifestyle he had engineered for them, an arrangement that had functioned smoothly for more than three decades.

He'd taken control from the beginning, setting the rules that governed her life even while she was entirely unaware of his existence. And the most important rule -- the one that kept them safe from a meddling world -- was to *stay the fuck away from people!* Well, she'd broken that one and her art student friend had paid the price.

Killing her was an easier task than he'd expected. In fact, he found the experience rather enjoyable. Not so much the physical act of burying the blade in her flesh, or the sight of all that blood rushing from her wounds. That was all very dramatic and exhilarating, but it was the look on the poor girl's face that really turned him on. The initial fear in her eyes, followed by the sudden realisation that she was about to die, and finally, that last silent plea, as she was desperately trying to hold on, to please, *please* allow her to live. It was the complete and utter power he wielded over her in those last impassioned moments that excited Aleksi. It made him feel alive.

He'd learned over the years to monitor his sister's behaviour day and night, even while in his dormant state. Rarely did he need to intervene directly, but there had been a number of times when circumstances required him to quickly take control in order to prevent Ula from doing something stupid. On this particular occasion -- the night that he destroyed her equipment -- he was roused when he became aware of a whispered phone call.

"...is that Detective Boyd?"

"Yes, this is Boyd. Who is this?"

"It's Ula Mishkin... You gave me your card and said I could phone anytime..."

"Oh, yes... Ms. Mishkin... Is everything all right?"

All sorts of alarms were going off in Aleksi's mind, warning him of the pending danger, but like someone waking from an uncomfortable dream, it took him a moment to find his way to the surface.

"I... I don't know," Ula continued, her voice trembling. *"But, I... I think someone is in the house and... I think it might be -- "*

She went suddenly silent as Aleksi emerged and took control. There was a moment when it seemed as though Ula would resist, but, in the end, she meekly surrendered and put herself away, as she always did. Aleksi looked around to find himself in her bedroom, cowering behind the locked door.

"Ms. Mishkin?" Boyd said. "Are you still there?"

"Yes... Yes, I'm here," Aleksi replied in Ula's voice. "I'm sorry, I... I feel rather foolish now... phoning you at this hour... I don't know what I was saying earlier, but everything is fine now. Just fine."

"You said there might be an intruder in the house..."

"Did I? Oh, well, I... I must have been dreaming. Sleepwalking. I often do that. But I'm awake now and everything is perfectly fine."

"You're certain?"

"Yes. I'm quite sure, thank you."

"Would you like me to send a patrol car?"

"Oh, no. That really won't be necessary."

"If you feel under threat -- "

"Everything is fine, detective. Really. Thank you. Goodbye!"

Aleksi hung up and stood there, quietly brooding. Whatever was he going to do with his uncontrollable alter ego? She was his sister, after all, and he felt a certain fondness for her, but from the moment that pretty young thing stepped through the door she'd become obsessed, and there was simply no room for three in their relationship. Aleksi believed that by removing the girl he would remove the problem, but in the end, it had only made matters worse.

Retreating from his sister's bedroom, which always made him feel slightly uncomfortable, Aleksi bounded down the stairs and retrieved the key to the cellar door from behind the fridge, where he kept it hidden from Ula. His sanctuary, which he'd set up as a teenager using the old furnishings from the lockup, was located in a dark, underground cavern at the back of the basement. It was a small space accommodating a single bed, a chest of drawers, a wardrobe, and his most recent addition, a large antique hope chest, painted in a faded floral pattern, which he was using for temporary storage. The adjoining bathroom, with toilet, washbasin, and old cast iron tub, had been installed a few years earlier, as a twenty-first birthday present to himself, releasing him from the need to be constantly cleaning up after himself so as to avoid arousing Ula's suspicions.

Stepping up to the gilded mirror that hung above the sink, he leaned in close and inspected his reflection. It was still her face at the moment. Plain features, grey complexion, and dull, lifeless eyes. It suited Ula, but ultimately, like her mousy personality, it was deadly boring. His persona, on the other hand, required a bit of flair.

"You know we're in this together," he said as he reached for his makeup kit. "If I go to prison, you go with me."

He often spoke directly to Ula while she was sleeping. Although she was unaware of his words, perhaps they would filter down, he thought, and subliminally influence her behaviour, which was becoming more and more erratic with each passing day. At any rate, it was a way to break the silence, which he found unbearably oppressive.

"You and your idiotic fantasies," he continued. "I mean, really! A house by the sea?" Pinning his hair back, he began his metamorphosis with a thin layer of liquid foundation. "I'm sure the idea of hiding out in another coma suits you down to the ground, but for god's sake, I could never let you put us back there! Even if you can't remember, I do. All that awful black emptiness! Christ! We might as well be fucking dead!"

A bit of blush, some liner and mascara to highlight the eyes, and Ula began to disappear. A touch of tinted lip gloss, a dose of hair gel and the transformation was complete. Aleksi stood back to admire his work and smiled. He was himself again.

Ula's twin brother was everything she could never be. Self-assured and uninhibited, with a restless nature, he escaped the oppressive walls of the Highbury house at every opportunity. Hitting a late-night club, crashing an art opening, or just walking Soho's busy streets, he was happy anywhere he could get lost in a crowd. See and be seen, that was his creed. And if you're going to be seen, be seen at your best. Looking though his extensive wardrobe, he decided that black on black suited his mood on this night.

Ula's rebellious behaviour had been a concern for some time, but it came to a head on the day she agreed to allow that German to start rummaging around in the girl's memory. His sister's meanderings could be steered away from dangerous revelations, but if the scientist had found his way to the night of the killing... well, it simply couldn't be allowed.

Then there was the ridiculous idea of leaving the city to live out some solitary fantasy while he was stuck in a permanent drug-induced coma. How oppressive! And now she was making panicked phone calls in the middle of the night to the fucking detective in charge of the case! His dear sister was simply becoming much too unpredictable and far too dangerous. Something had to be done.

Ironically, it was Ula herself who provided the solution. Aleksi was at first horrified by her plan to sell the house and he had every intention of sabotaging her dream. But after a bit of reflection, he realised that it could provide the perfect way out for him. He would let her proceed with the sale and once the money was in the bank, instead of allowing her to take them off to some boring seaside cottage, he would put her to sleep while they made a different, more far-flung journey. There were several appealing options, but Aleksi's choice had been obvious from the start. After all, Rio de Janeiro was the undisputed party capital of the world.

He smiled at the thought of Ula waking up on some Brazilian beach, surrounded by all that bare skin, with no idea where she was or how she got there. The poor girl, she'd be so confused. He might even introduce himself to her at that point. He would tell her everything, from the beginning, then he'd say a fond farewell and put her down for good.

Aleksi wasn't a fool. He had long ago surmised that Ula had created him following his own unfortunate demise at the hand of their mother, and while he was grateful, he couldn't let sentimentality stand in the way of his own interests. Content that the future finally looked promising, he retired to the sitting room where he sat at the piano and, by candlelight, played his favourite piece -- *Moonlight Sonata* by Ludwig von Beethoven.

39.

"Something wrong, darling?"

Leonard found Boyd standing in the middle of the room, phone in hand, looking a bit perplexed.

"No, no." She shook her head and tried to smile. "Just a rather odd phone call."

"Who in god's name is ringing you at this hour?" He placed a tray containing tea and toast on the coffee table.

"Ula Mishkin," Boyd replied absentmindedly, preoccupied with her thoughts.

"Who?"

"Oh... She was Mia Fraser's landlady."

"Mia Fraser?"

The name was familiar, but in spite of their earlier conversation, Leonard couldn't quite make the connection.

"The girl who was murdered," Boyd reminded him. "On Highbury Field."

"Oh, yes, the American girl. I remember now. Of course. Tragic." He settled into his armchair and took a cautious sip of the hot liquid. "Why would her landlady be phoning you up in the middle of the night? Is it something to do with the case?"

"No. At least I don't think so. She thought someone had broken into her house."

"She needs to be ringing emergency services, not you." He took a bite of heavily buttered toast.

"Yes, well, seems that it was a false alarm anyway."

"Sit down, sweetheart. Have some toast. I put Marmite on yours."

Boyd sat on the sofa and picked up a piece of toast, but had second thoughts and put it back on the plate. "She changed her story halfway through the call. Said that she'd imagined it."

"People imagine a lot of things in the dead of night."

"Claimed that she'd been sleepwalking."

"You don't sound convinced."

Boyd shrugged. "I don't know. Just a feeling. Perhaps I'm wrong."

"But perhaps not."

"It's probably nothing."

Leonard leaned forward and gave his daughter a knowing look. "Remember what I told you about listening to your gut?"

"Yes, of course, but -- "

"Your gut is crying out to you right now, sweetheart."

Boyd frowned and didn't reply for a moment. She reached for her tea and took a sip. "I suppose it wouldn't do any harm to go down and have a look. Just to confirm that everything's all right."

"No harm whatsoever." Leonard brushed the crumbs off his hands and stood up. "I can be dressed and ready to go in five."

"Dad -- "

He put his hand up to cut her off. "Listen, sweetheart. If you expect me to sit here on me own, drinking tea and eating burnt toast in my pyjamas at five o'clock in the morning, you need to think again. Now I promise that I'll sit quietly in the car while you see what's up with your landlady, and after that I just might decide to show you where to get the best egg and bacon sarnie in

London. And not only that..." He gave her a wink. "...if you play your cards right, I might even buy you one."

40.

Making the turn onto Highbury Crescent, Boyd pulled the car to the kerb and killed the engine. "I won't be long," she said, glancing over at Leonard as she unbuckled her seatbelt.

"Don't worry, darling. I'm not going anywhere."

"Shall I leave the radio on for you?"

"No, I'll be fine."

As she stepped into the pre-dawn mist, Boyd became aware of the muted sound of someone playing a piano. Growing in clarity as she went through the gate and climbed the steps to the front entrance, she paused to listen, not wanting to interrupt what seemed, to her, a flawless rendition of *Moonlight Sonata.*

Looking out across the park where Mia Fraser had lost her life, Boyd felt something in the air -- a vibration that seemed to charge the atmosphere, quickening the pulse and heightening the senses. But perhaps the tension wasn't in the air, she thought. Perhaps it was in her. In the end, it didn't matter. Whatever the source of her disquiet, she felt anxious and on edge.

As the composition came to a haunting conclusion, Boyd took a deep breath and stepped forward to ring the bell. A long silence followed, then a sudden movement in the bay window. She turned, just in time to catch a fleeting glimpse of a face, but it abruptly pulled away, withdrawing behind a set of thick velvet drapes.

She waited, stomach churning as the time passed. One minute. Then two, three, and four. Five minutes and still no one appeared at the door. Was she being ignored, or was there something terribly wrong inside the house?

Moving around to the side of the property, Boyd checked the windows and peered over the back wall into the garden, but found no discernible sign of a break in. As she retraced her steps to the front of the building, she thought she saw another movement in the window -- a rustling of the curtains -- but perhaps it was nothing. It was too dark to be certain.

Moving into the dim light of a street lamp, Boyd considered her options. There was no point in ringing the bell again, but she needed some kind of assurance that nothing was amiss. If she spoke to Mishkin again, she could leave feeling confident that she wasn't in danger. But as she retrieved her phone from a jacket pocket, Boyd heard the loud *CLICK* of the front door opening.

"Ms. Mishkin...?"

She called out, but there was no response. Mounting the steps to the entrance, she tried again.

"Ms. Mishkin? Are you there?"

Still no reply. Pushing gently on the door, it swung open. She took a tentative step inside, peered into the darkness, and called out for a third time.

"Ms. Mishkin? It's Detective Inspector Boyd... Is everything all right?"

Still no response. Taking another few steps, she peeked into the sitting room. A solitary candle burned atop the piano, its silky flame providing the only illumination in the house. Locating a light switch on the wall, Boyd flicked it up and down a couple of times, but to no effect. The electricity was out.

With growing concern, she switched her phone's flashlight on and carefully made her way toward the back of the house.

"Ms. Mishkin! I know you're here! I saw you in the window!"

But was it Ula she'd seen? Boyd began to doubt her own memory. It was so brief and it was so dark. Perhaps -- like so many of the eyewitnesses she'd interviewed -- her assumptions had coloured her perception.

"Ms. Mishkin!" she repeated as she entered the kitchen. "Please respond if you can hear me! I need to know that you're safe!"

There was a brief silence, then Ula's muffled voice called out. "I'm in the cellar! Come down!"

Boyd's heart beat a little faster as she moved warily forward, using the faint beam of the phone to light her path. Locating an open door on the kitchen's back wall, she peered down a set of steep wooden steps into the building's dark depths.

"Ms. Mishkin?"

"Yes, I'm down here." The voice echoed off the stone walls, making it difficult to pinpoint its origin. "The electricity has gone out and I can't seem to find the circuit breakers."

Boyd hesitated. It didn't feel right. "Move into my light so I can see you!" she said.

There was a pause before Aleksi replied, still using Ula's voice. "I... I can't, I... I've lost my cane in the darkness! Please come down with your light! I need your help!"

Boyd hesitated another moment, then took hold of the rail and cautiously descended into the dank cold of the basement.

"Where are you?" she called out.

"To your left! Follow my voice... Yes, that's it. You're getting closer. Almost there..."

As Boyd edged nearer, hunching over to pass beneath the wooden beams of the low-slung ceiling, her light revealed a stone archway that seemed to lead into a small vaulted chamber.

"Ms. Mishkin?"

"Yes... Keep coming..." The voice reverberated. "I'm in here."

Stepping through the arch, Boyd found an arrangement of furnishings that looked to her like an old-fashioned prison cell. A single wrought iron bed, a chest of drawers, a wardrobe, and, somewhat incongruously, a large hand-painted hope chest. As she moved the light across the antique's faded floral designs, which seemed to be of Russian origin, she noticed a dark stain on the stone floor beneath it. The pattern suggested that the leak -- whatever it was -- had emanated from inside the box. Moving closer, she knelt down and held the phone's beam a few inches above the mark. Dark brown and slightly sticky, it was impossible to be certain, but it looked and felt very much like blood.

Boyd quickly stood up and swept the surrounding darkness with her light. "Ms. Mishkin..? Are you there..?"

No response.

Feeling suddenly vulnerable and sensing that she'd walked into a trap, Boyd swiped her finger across the phone's screen and dialled 999 -- only to realise that there was no signal in the underground chamber. Heart beating wildly, she knew she couldn't panic. Keep your head and think, she told herself.

"Ms. Mishkin..."

Boyd called out once again as she lifted the chest's heavy wooden lid. "...I want you to know that I've just called for back-up! Officers will be arriving very shortly!"

Silence.

Turning the light into the box's dark interior, Boyd braced for what she would find. But nothing could have prepared her for the sight of Erik's blood-stained corpse, shoved into the chest in a twisted mess of broken arms and tangled legs. His dead blue eyes seemed to be staring directly at her.

Stumbling backward, Boyd sensed a movement and turned, but too late. Aleksi stepped out of the darkness, swung the cane, and the world disappeared.

41.

Leonard was drifting again. Lost in a reverie, the pictures that spilled out of his mind, like water from a faulty container, were more vivid, more real than his everyday reality. It was a private world that he alone could access, and it often made him smile.

The sky was as blue as blue could be, the air so clear that you could see halfway across the channel to the white cliffs of Dover. Grace had to hold her hat in place so the wind wouldn't take it and he was having trouble lighting his pipe. With the deck all to themselves, it felt like they were the only two people in the world.

"Paris is fine," he said, leaning onto the railing. "But it's good to see home again."

"Perhaps we'll go back one day," Grace replied.

"Why not?" Leonard smiled and lit yet another match.

"I'd love to see the Parthenon, too," she mused.

"There's nothing to stop us, is there?"

Grace shook her head. "You always say that."

"Well, it's true."

"I know you mean it, darling but, well... "

"But what?"

"You work so hard. Such long hours. I'm not blaming you, but I feel like we hardly see each other any more, let alone find time for a holiday."

Leonard turned to his wife and frowned. "But Grace, don't you know? Those days are over. I thought I told you. I'm a free man now. No responsibilities. I can come and go as I please."

Grace nodded, but she seemed a little bit saddened by the news. "Well then," she replied. "I suppose that means we'll be able do all the things that we always wanted to do."

"Absolutely!" Leonard agreed wholeheartedly. "The Parthenon, the pyramids, the bloody Hanging Gardens of Babylon! We'll see them all! Not even the sky's the limit for us now!"

"That's marvellous." Grace smiled, but he could see that something was still bothering her.

"What is it? What's wrong?" he asked.

"Oh, it's nothing. It all sounds wonderful. It's just that..."

"What, love?"

"I'm worried about Sarah."

"Sarah? Why are you worried about her?"

"Well, she's been gone quite a long time."

"Has she?"

"Yes, she has. Perhaps it would be a good idea if you went to check on her."

Leonard nodded and, as the dream dissipated, replaced by the cold January dawn, he needed a moment to get his bearings. Looking over at the house on Highbury Crescent, he saw that the front door was wide open.

42.

Boyd opened her eyes to find her wrists and ankles tightly bound, her mouth sealed with gaffer's tape, and water rising all around her. Kneeling beside the cast iron tub where she lay, Aleksi cocked his head and produced a smile.

"They say that drowning is quite a pleasant way to die," he said, voice quivering with nervous energy. "But I don't see how they could possibly know that. I mean, it's not as if anyone can report back, is it?"

Boyd tried to sit up, but Aleksi gently pushed her back down into the water and held her there with one hand.

"I don't believe it can be true, though," he continued. "I mean, really. How could it be a pleasant experience to choke and sputter and desperately gasp for air as water slowly fills your lungs? It would probably be more accurate to say that it's one of the less painful ways to die." He shrugged his shoulders. "At any rate, it will be interesting to watch."

The panic in Boyd's eyes gave Aleksi a rush of excitement. He had nothing in particular against her, but on the other hand, he had no sympathy for her, either. This would be his third killing and he was beginning to think it would become a regular feature of his life.

"This must be confusing for you," he said. "Well, allow me to introduce myself. My name is Aleksi and, yes, I'm the one you've been looking for. I killed that young girl in the park. With this..."

Gripped in his right hand was a large butcher's knife. "I used it on that scientist, too. The one you saw in the chest." He leaned in close and lowered his voice, as if sharing an intimate secret. "You may have noticed that it wasn't all that easy to get him in there. I had to rearrange him a bit, if you know what I mean."

Assessing the water level, which was enveloping Boyd's shoulders now, Aleksi considered pointing out that she had only another few minutes to live, but decided there was no need to state the obvious. And besides, he preferred to focus on himself.

"You might be thinking that I won't get away with it," he said. "But that's the beauty of my situation. You see, in your world, I'm no more than a figment of my sister's twisted imagination. I don't exist." He smiled again. "And it's very difficult to find someone who doesn't exist. As you know only too well!"

Boyd tried desperately to speak through her gag, but it was garbled and Aleksi chose to ignore her.

"My point," he continued, "...is that my sister will take the blame for all these killings, not me. And they'll never find her, either, because, well... let's just say I have plans for Ula, too." He used the knife to point to his own head. "She's in here now. Sleeping like a baby, with no idea about any of this."

The water was covering Boyd's entire torso now, lapping up around her chin. She tried to sit up again, but Aleksi kept her in place.

"It'll be easier for you if you don't struggle," he said. "Although I can certainly understand why you would. It's only natural to fight for your life." He sighed and shook his head in appreciation of the moment. "What must be going through your mind right now? Is your life flashing before your eyes? Or are you still hoping that you'll find some way to escape? As they say, hope springs eternal!"

Boyd understood that her chances of survival were dim, but she also knew that her one remaining hope was to somehow engage this sick individual. Closing her eyes, she dug deep to find the strength to maintain her composure while every every cell in her body was telling her to resist with everything she had. Aleksi felt her body relax and saw that the fear was gone from her eyes when she opened them. She looked inexplicably peaceful, and he didn't like it.

"You do know what's happening, don't you?" he blurted out. "You're about to die a fucking horrible death!"

Whatever words Boyd spoke through her gag were equally calm and they aroused Aleksi's curiosity.

"Oh, you have something to say, do you? All right then..." He started to remove the tape from her mouth, but hesitated. "I hope you don't think that screaming will do you any good," he said. "It certainly didn't help that scientist."

Boyd shook her head, as if to promise her silence, and Aleksi ripped the gag off her face. "There!" he said. "Go ahead! Speak! Blow me away with your last words! Make it something wonderfully profound!"

"I want to speak to Ula," Boyd said, her voice steady and strong.

Aleksi tried to laugh it off, but it threw him. "Ula's not available," he said, with a hint of resentment. "I'm afraid you're stuck with me."

"Ula, if you can hear me, please wake up!"

"Don't do that," Aleksi said, growing agitated.

"I know you're in there, Ula! You must wake up!"

"Stop saying that!"

"Ula!" Boyd called out with increasing urgency as the water continued to rise, splashing into her mouth. "Wake up and look at me!"

Feeling his sister stir, Aleksi stood up and took a step backward. "Oh, no," he said, shaking his head. "No, you don't!"

"I know you can hear me, Ula!" Boyd cried out. "You need to wake up now!"

Leaning over the tub, Aleksi clamped his free hand over Boyd's mouth and brandished the knife with the other, holding the blade threatening close to the underside of her neck.

"I told you to stop saying that!"

Unable to breathe, Boyd bit down hard, taking a piece of skin and muscle out of Aleksi's palm. He sprung to his feet, howling with pain.

"BITCH!" he shrieked.

"Ula!" Boyd frantically called out as the water continued to rise. "Wake up, Ula!"

"No!" Sensing his sister emerging from her sleep, Aleksi panicked. "No, you don't!"

"Ula!" Boyd persisted. "Wake up and take control!"

Aleksi flew into a rage. Falling to his knees, he stabbed at the rising water in a frenzied, incoherent attack. The first two thrusts missed the target, but the third found Boyd's chest. Cutting deep, the blade sliced through muscle and bone, finally piercing the upper portion of her left lung. Crying out in pain, she slipped back into the tub, gasping for air as blood surged into the bath water, transforming it into a sickly pink colour.

Feeling spent, Aleksi stood up, took a deep, shaky breath, and drank the moment in with silent appreciation. He wondered if Boyd would die by drowning or might she bleed to death first? She was still breathing, but just barely. It was tempting to push her head down under the water and hold it there, see if she would struggle. But no, he told himself. Be patient. It won't take long for that vacant look to appear. Stand back and let it happen.

As Boyd slipped down below the water line, she looked at peace now. Aleksi wondered if there was a clear line between life and death, or if it was more indefinite than that.

43.

Leonard came out of nowhere. Charging through the darkness, he launched himself across the room and tackled Aleksi from behind, taking him down onto the hard stone floor. Adrenalin surging, he was suddenly as clear and as strong as he'd been four decades earlier, fresh off the course at the Met training centre. Wrapping his legs around Aleksi's torso, he got him in a chokehold, arched his back and tightened his grip, creating pressure on the carotid artery. It took just a few seconds for him to go limp.

Leaping to his feet, Leonard moved quickly and efficiently, plunging his arms into the now overflowing tub, grasping his lifeless daughter and pulling her up, out of the water. Clutching her in his arms, he carefully lowered her onto the floor and quickly removed the gaffer's tape from her wrists.

"Hold on, sweetheart," he whispered as he applied pressure to the wound with one hand and began chest compressions with the other. "One... two... three... Breathe!" Leaning in, he gave her the kiss of life. "Come on, darling! One... two... three... Breathe!"

But she was unresponsive.

"Come on!" His voice quivered, betraying his rising emotions. "One... two... three... Breathe!"

Still nothing.

"Don't you do this, Sarah!" he cried. "Don't you dare do this! One... two... three... Breath!"

There was a movement.

"That's it, sweetheart! Now breathe! Come on! Breathe!"

A choking sound.

"Open your eyes, sweetheart! Open your eyes and breathe!"

Boyd began to cough and sputter, then her eyes fluttered open. She turned her head to the side, expelling blood and water onto the floor.

"Thank god," Leonard said, trying to hold back his tears as he removed his jacket and placed it over her. "Thank god."

"Dad..."

"Don't try to speak, sweetheart. We'll get you to the hospital as quick as -- "

The look in Boyd's eyes stopped him cold. He spun around to find Aleksi standing over them, knife in hand. Springing to his feet, he prepared for another attack -- but something had changed. Something elusive, but undeniable. The aggressor, full of angry hostility, was gone and in his place stood someone quite different.

"Ula?" Boyd whispered. "Is that you?"

She looked from Leonard to Boyd, then to the bloodied knife. "Did I... Did I do this?"

"No... " Boyd struggled to get the words out. "It wasn't you. It was Aleksi."

Ula frowned and shook her head, as if trying to fight off an excruciating pain. "I... I don't understand," she cried.

But the truth was, she did understand. While never fully aware of the fault line that existed in her psyche, somewhere deep down, in the depths of her subconscious, she knew about Aleksi. In a way, she'd been his accomplice -- or at least his facilitator -- granting him the power to manipulate her, to use and abuse her.

As a child, she'd given him life, perhaps out of some sense of guilt, or fear, or maybe it was just sheer loneliness. It probably started with a whispered conversation in the dark, young Ula taking on the role of her missing brother, speaking for him and then, as they grew older, thinking for him and, finally, acting for him. As Aleksi blossomed, Ula shrunk further into herself, allowing her brother to voice all the contempt and self-loathing she felt for herself and, ultimately, she became little more than a front for her long dead brother.

Then came Mia. Ula's unfulfilled need for human contact -- for love -- had finally found a receptacle in the charming young girl with the soft southern accent. But, like everything else in her tragic life, it gave her nothing but pain. And now, as she gazed into the gilded mirror above the sink, she finally met her twin, and she understood everything, including what he had done.

"Ula...?"

Transfixed, Ula didn't respond.

"Ula...?" Boyd repeated, summoning her strength. "Look at me, Ula."

She seemed to be lost, someplace far away.

"There are people who can help you, Ula," Boyd said, her voice barely a whisper. "Let us help you."

A long silence hung in the room. Then Ula's face became contorted and she shook her head, vehemently. "No!" she cried out. *"NO!"*

"Ula?"

"He's coming... he's coming back!"

"Fight him, Ula! Fight back!"

"I... I can't... he's... he's too strong!"

Leonard took a tentative step toward her. "Give me the knife," he said gently, reaching his hand out. "Everything will be all right if you give me the knife."

Ula was paralysed, unsure what to do.

"Give it to him, Ula..." Boyd pleaded. "Give the knife to my father. Please, Ula..."

For a moment it seemed that she was going to give up the weapon. But she hesitated. "If he wakes up..." she whispered. "If he wakes up I don't know what he'll do."

Without another word, she took the knife in both hands and turned it on herself. Before Leonard could move, Ula closed her eyes and plunged the blade into her heart.

Leonard tried, of course, but there was no saving her. The wound was just too deep.

44.

The darkness didn't frighten her. Not this time.

Sitting up, young Ula, six years old, looked out across the room and saw that Aleksi wasn't in his bed. But she knew where to find him. Slipping out from under the covers, she walked barefoot, following the light to the bathroom.

The sight of her mother dangling from the ceiling didn't upset her, not like the first time. This time she didn't cry, or hide in the corner until the men came to take her away. And this time she knew better than to look up at her mother's face. She went straight to the bathtub, where she knew she would find Aleksi. He looked so peaceful, she thought, lying there, immersed in the warm water. As if he was sleeping.

The tub was too high to clamber over so she retrieved the bin from under the sink and turned it upside down to use as a stepping stool. Climbing up and over, she slipped into the tub and took her place beside her brother.

His hand was icy cold when she took it in hers, but it still gave her the comfort she was seeking. They had promised each other that they would be together, forever and ever, come what may.

Now they would be.

45.

"Knock, knock..."

Whittington Hospital was a labyrinth of interconnected buildings and long corridors that seemed to lead everywhere but where he was going, so Nichols was pleased that he'd finally found the right room. Boyd was sitting up in bed, watching something on her iPad.

"Oh, hello there!" She greeted him with a warm smile as she removed her ear buds. "Gosh! What a surprise!"

Nichols stepped into the room and quickly noted that Leonard was sitting at the far end of the room, staring out the window at a grey London skyline.

"Oh..." He paused. "Am I intruding?"

Boyd shook her head. "No, no, come in. He's been like that for a while. I thought it best to leave him."

Nichols nodded and remembered the flowers he'd been carrying around. "Oh! I brought you these... Roses."

"That's very thoughtful. Thank you."

"Looks like you've got quite a few admirers," he said, noting that the room was overflowing with floral arrangements.

"Yes, well, I don't know most of them. Hardly any, in fact."

"The price of fame." Nichols smiled, a little uneasily. "Shall I add these to the collection?"

"No, no... I, ah... They're beautiful... I'll keep them here, by the bed."

Nichols filled an empty glass with water from the bathroom and placed the bouquet on the table at Boyd's side. "They're winter roses," he explained. "From my garden."

"Really?"

Nichols shrugged. "It's kind of a hobby."

"I'm impressed."

"You should see the Peruvian Lilys."

"Wow. Sounds exotic."

"Oh, yes. Very."

"Well, then. I guess you'd better invite me over."

"Consider it done," Nichols beamed.

Boyd invited him to pull up a chair and the two detectives soon lost track of time, talking about everything and nothing for the rest of the afternoon. Through it all, Leonard sat by the window, engrossed in whatever adventure he and Grace were having, a wry smile affixed to his face.

*   *   *

About the Author

Tom Gabbay was born in 1953 in Bloomington, Indiana. After studying painting in London and Philadelphia, he began his career in New York, producing award-winning animated short films for the well known children's program *Sesame Street*. During his tenure at NBC Entertainment he served as a Director of Children's Programs, Director of Comedy Programs, and Creative Director for NBC Europe. In addition to his novels, he has written several screenplays and contributed political cartoons to the Philadelphia Daily News.

http://www.tomgabbay.com

<u>Praise For Tom Gabbay's Previous Work</u>

"Powered by relentless pacing and a story line abounding in subterfuge, treachery and subversion, this Ludlumesque page-turner offers invaluable historical insights into the turbulent relationship between America ("the Great Satan") and Iran."

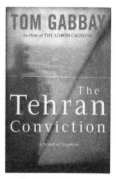

- Publisher's Weekly on **"The Tehran Conviction"**

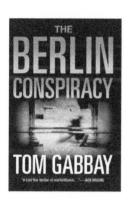

"A Cold War thriller of real brilliance; John le Carré with a witty ironic edge that will start you thinking about the real truth behind the Kennedy assassination."

- Jack Higgins on **"The Berlin Conspiracy"**

"Gabbay serves it all up with Raymond Chandler--esque dark humor, a rich sense of place and a fine feel for the yawning chasm between those privileged to float above the exigencies of that dark time and those who were engulfed in its horrors."

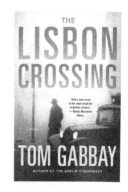

- Forbes on **"The Lisbon Crossing"**

CPSIA information can be obtained
at www.ICGtesting.com
Printed in the USA
LVHW090546180420
653952LV00002B/720